GIRL AT THE BOTTOM OF THE SEA

McSWEENEY'S
McMULLENS

McSweeney's McMullens publishes great new books—and new editions
of out-of-print classics—for individuals and families of all kinds.

McSweeney's is a privately held company with wildly fluctuating resources.
McSweeney's McMullens and colophon are copyright © 2012 McSweeney's & McMullens.

Printed in the United States.

2   4   6   8   10   9   7   5   3   1

ISBN: 978-1-940450-00-1

www.mcsweeneys.net

GIRL
AT THE
BOTTOM OF
THE SEA

Michelle Tea

To Chloe Lark.

Chapter 1

It's like a fist, Sophie thought. A giant fist the color of water, which is the color of nothing, but gray-blue like the cloudy sky and black from the oil and grease of the creek. Being water the great wave shone, catching a sliver of fiery orange from the last bit of sun in the sky. It was a terrible, liquid fist edged in burning colors, a shimmering, wet fireball smelling like the salt of the sea and the dirt of it, too.

Beneath the waters of the shallow creek, her face buried in Syrena's long hair, Sophie struggled. Syrena clutched her tighter, her strength surprising, magic and animal. But Sophie was not trying to escape, she only wanted to see. If she was going to die at the ocean hand of her grandmother, Sophie wanted to do it bravely.

Twisting her face free, she tilted it upward through the water, toward its grainy surface. Above her, the shadow of the great wave darkened the creek and Sophie could hear, muffled by the water and by her terror, shouts and screams from the shore. *Angel. Dr. Chen.* They would be running now, pushing through the torn links that fenced the creek, booking it for higher ground. *A tsunami in Chelsea Creek.* The rogue wave had reached its maximum height. All through the city, people would blink, rub their eyes, and shake their heads. Something tall and shining in the darkness—was it a cloud? It was nothing. It was gone as soon as they saw it. But the sound of it! The flooding on the banks!

When Kishka's mighty fist came down, Sophie felt herself fall to pieces. Though the pain was too great to fully comprehend, it was as if her body had become liquid inside and her bones and muscles were being ground into the trash and silt beneath her feet. She felt the mermaid torn away from her, thrown up into the sky. And before she could cry out, Sophie was flying, too. As hard as she had been punched down into the creek bed, so did the force of the wave catapult her into the air.

By the last light of the sky and the faraway streetlamps ringing the housing projects, Sophie and the very creek took flight. A shopping cart whizzed by, a car door, a small refrigerator. Like a girl in a horrible snow globe, she was suspended in a confetti of creek mud, stuck here and there with rocks, with bits of brick and chunks of cement. From her vantage she could see across all of Chelsea—the old-fashioned dome of City Hall, the red-and-white-checked water tower at the top of Soldier's Home, the Tobin Bridge like a length of green Legos, stretching into Boston, and even Boston itself, with its glittering buildings. And all around it, water.

Time seemed to slow as Sophie flew above the city and she looked down upon it. How small Chelsea looked, how tender it suddenly seemed, with its twinkling streetlights, the yellowy glow coming through the windows while inside families ate dinner, oblivious. Even the groups of boys gathered in the city square, the ones who had so often yelled after Sophie and forced her to take a different route home, seemed innocent to her now for all they didn't know. They thought that Chelsea was simply a city, a banged-up urban playground that held and trapped them. They had no idea that it was so much more—the birthplace for an ancient magic that had suddenly and powerfully awoken, a magic that was inside Sophie, that threaded through her family, coming down from her ancient and terrible grandmother who seemed to have become the poisoned creek itself and was now sending her granddaughter so many miles above the town that it looked like a child's toy beneath her, its graffitied walls and trash-strewn curbs no longer visible.

But at Sophie's wild height, with time slowing down around her as she tumbled from the sky, with all that she had learned racing through her head, Sophie saw only home. *What a strange way to leave home for the first time*, she thought as she flew. Her heart rang out for this town that had bugged her so hard, its packs of boys that menaced her, its dirty creek and beat-up parks. *It's mine*, she thought. *Mine to protect and return to. Mine to save—from my grandmother.*

At that thought, the wave that had lifted Sophie so violently into the air shattered around her like glass, and in every drip and drop, every splash, were the many faces of Kishka: Kishka the dragon, Kishka the grandmother. Kishka the young beauty and Kishka the swirling darkness, the very fabric of terror, the power that every act of evil draws its energy from. Kishka the *Odmieńce*—one of the last of these magical beings that walked the earth at the beginning of time, that had shaped the earth, the people and their ways. Kishka had shaped the world in the most terrible of ways, bringing war and pain and hatred. Kishka had been living off humanity's misery since the dawn of time; she'd grown rich with it, parked in a garbage dump in Chelsea, Massachusetts, passing her days as a cranky old woman. But now Kishka's secret was out. Sophie knew what her grandmother really was, and she knew that her own magic, whatever it may be, came from her. And now Sophie, with her little chunk of inherited magic, was going to have to face off with her grandmother, who had it all, whose magic was millennia-old.

And then there was Syrena.

The mermaid was flying through the night sky alongside her, a miracle of the air now, not the sea. For a moment Sophie forgot her own self—broken, hurled, imperiled—and was mesmerized by the sight of the creature, her first clear view. Her tail was so long! Thick and strong, it beat against the air as if Syrena was trying to swim through the sky. Her scales in places glinted like rhinestones, and in others they were dull, torn up, trailing ragged tendrils. Her long, pale arms looked made from the moon that glowed in the sky, and they scratched and flailed at the darkness. Her hair streamed out behind her, longer even than her tail, impossible. It looked like a great mat of seaweed, its own ecosystem, stuck with seashells and tiny sea creatures and woven through with slick green sea plants. At the mermaid's hips were strange, winglike fins; like a jellyfish they undulated. Syrena curled her body through

the air, but she was not a bird, she was a sea creature. And as Sophie felt herself begin to plummet, so too did the mermaid.

Syrena flipped herself in the air like a wild acrobat. "Like me!" she screamed to Sophie, the rush of the fall ripping the words from her mouth, but Sophie caught them. Syrena had tumbled her body into a dive and stretched her arms before her. Her head was tucked, her hair tangled around her face like a mask. Even if Sophie wasn't so broken, she doubted she'd be able to do as Syrena showed her. Clumsy Sophie, who'd kicked her gymnastics teacher in the chin during her first (and last) class. Sophie, probably the only person on earth not to have a center of gravity. Sophie who wobbled and tripped even when her shoelaces were tied; Sophie would not have been able to flip her body into the arrow that Syrena had become, cleaving the water, sending up a great spray. No. Even if she could have moved, Sophie would have entered the water the same way: in a terrible back flop that would have turned her bones to jelly—if she still had bones. But Sophie didn't think she had bones anymore. She was a beanbag, a water balloon. She hit the water with a tremendous impact, and then she sank into the darkness.

Chapter 2

Some time later, Sophie awoke under the water. The talisman she wore around her neck softly illuminated the rippling area closest to her. Even the watery fist of her grandmother—as big, it seemed, as the ocean itself—had not been enough to rip the sea glass from her neck. It was strong, just like Angel, who had given it to her. Unable to move, Sophie thought of Angel hard at work in Kishka's dump, working the glass tumbler with thick, dirty gloves on her hands, hoisting barrels of sparkling color onto her shoulders, her brow sweating beneath the band of the woolly cap she wore no matter the weather. Sophie wished she could reach out to her friend's mind to let her know she was okay, but then, Sophie wasn't sure she was okay. But if she was going to be okay she knew that the talisman would help her, and she thanked Angel in her heart as she lay inside its cool, blue glow.

The light attracted a small school of curious fish. They were nothing more than slivers, silvery and translucent. As one they darted toward

the glow, and as one they quickly twitched away. If Sophie had been able to move she could have reached out and touched them. Instead, she just watched their movements, all as one, as if conducted by a giant fish just out of sight, holding a baton. The brave ones at the front of the school put their tiny fish mouths right onto the glass and ate the small bits of effluvia that had settled there. She wished she could communicate with them as she had with the pigeons of Chelsea, that she could expect a new group of English-speaking animals to join up with her wherever she went, helping her out like she was some urban Snow White. But Sophie knew the pigeons were special, with their sweetness and their fierceness, and how her heart ached for them as she lay there at the bottom of the bay. What Sophie would have given to listen to Arthur rage against Kishka then, at her terrible powers, at how she had made the creek come alive and turn against them all. Arthur would have some choice words for her grandmother, delivered in his husky squawk with much flapping of feathers. But as quickly as a tiny smile came to her lips, Sophie realized that Arthur's beloved Livia was gone—gone from all of them, forever. It probably wasn't spite Arthur was feeling right now. It was probably something much more heartbreaking.

Sophie sighed, a jellyfish-sized air bubble that shimmered up and away. She watched it travel, losing sight of it before it reached the surface. She could tell that she was deep, but not terribly so. In fact, she realized, it was the noise of what sounded like a party boat that had roused her. The dull thump of bad music and the shrill chorus of people yelling, hollering because the music was too loud or they were too drunk or both. *Booze cruises*, her mother called them. Sophie had seen them twinkling by on summer nights when she and her mom drove out to where the harbor sloshed up against Chelsea. To Sophie, they looked like toys; they looked fun. Her mother had dismissed them. "Just a bunch of drunk people," Andrea had said. "They pay a lot of money to get seasick and puke off the side of a boat." Sophie had made a gross joke about the harbor being filled with vomit, and Andrea indulged her with a laugh. The tinny sounds of a Madonna song wafted over them, gentle as the waves.

It had been a sweet moment, but now it made Sophie feel sad. Andrea probably would have loved to have gone on a booze cruise. She worked hard, with barely a day off. Days she didn't work she either ran errands for hours or conked out in front of the television, exhausted. Or both. Sophie didn't think she'd ever seen her mother get dressed up, flick a fan of frosty eye shadow above her eyes, and go dancing. She figured her mom probably wanted to so badly she'd made herself hate it. *When I'm done with saving humanity, I am going to make my mom go on a booze cruise*, Sophie vowed. She thought Ella would probably love such a thing too, and promised that when she reconnected with her best friend she wouldn't be such a nerd. She'd let Ella put makeup on her like she was one of those giant Barbie heads little girls smear fake lipstick onto. She'd let Ella do something with her head of snarls—even just detangling it would make Ella so happy. She'd ask her friend if she could borrow a pair of her jeans, one of her strappy tops, a pair of platform flip-flops. She'd suggest they go dancing at one of the awful underage dance clubs Ella always wanted to go to. They sounded horrible to Sophie—cheesy music, dumb boys with gelled hair trying to rub their hips on you on the dance floor, blinking lights making it hard to see, hard to focus— but for Ella she would do it. Sophie swore that if she got better and got out of the bay and back to Chelsea she would be a better friend.

If she got better, *if* she got back? Sophie's own thoughts sent a chill through her spine—or where her spine once was. Things had gotten so crazy, science-fiction crazy, action-movie crazy, that she really didn't know what was going to happen, just that somehow she was going to make it all better. She, the girl with the broken bones at the bottom of the bay, too scared to go to a teen dance club with her best friend: she was going to save the world from her grandmother's ancient evil.

At this thought, Sophie began to cry a little, tiny tears that squeezed out the sides of her eyes and became lost in the bay. She was *such* a baby. But she suddenly didn't care. She'd give anything to be back at home, huddled on the couch watching a dumb reality show beside her snoozing, overworked mom. If that made her a baby she didn't care. She wanted it so badly she could practically taste it, and it tasted like a bowl of cereal for dinner, milky and sweet.

She thought of sweet Hennie, her magical aunt. Hennie, working every day at the creepy old grocery store down the street, the store Sophie had avoided for so many years. She could have known Hennie for so much longer, could have learned so much magic from her! But Sophie had had no idea, and like everyone else she'd been scared of Hennie, Hennie who looked like a witch with her wild gray hair and craggy face. She wondered where Hennie was now, and what had happened to Laurie LeClair, the girl with the worst reputation in all of Chelsea. She had come into Hennie's grocery store possessed by the *Dola,* that destiny-policing creature, but when Sophie had left she was just herself, Laurie, cranky and messed-up and confused about where she was, with her screaming, neglected baby screaming and neglected by her side. Too much had happened, and look where it had left Sophie: lumped in the Boston Harbor, useless, cut off from everything and everyone. Not even in pain. That was what really scared her. She was too badly beaten by the fist of the creek not to be feeling any pain.

The coming and going of the school of silvery fish eventually lulled Sophie back into a sort of sleep; like a hypnotic pendulum, they danced back and forth around her necklace, and her eyes grew heavy. She imagined the flash of them leaping over the moon, full tonight, its bright beam cutting the water dimly. What would become of her? She was like a patch of weeds at the water's bottom, alive but immobile. Could she even speak? She tried. "Help," she spoke into the water. She repeated herself, louder. "Help." And louder again, "Help!" The fish startled away at the sound, moving as one, a silver cloud. Sophie closed her eyes. And when she opened them again, the mermaid was there.

Chapter 3

Of course Syrena would not approach gently. Pushed toward Sophie by the underwater waves of a too-close boat, the mermaid shook her fist and yelled curses in a language too ancient for Sophie to understand. Propelled by her powerful tail, Syrena came straight for Sophie, pulling the girl into her arms in one fluid scoop. Nestled in the mermaid's arms like a baby, Sophie noticed that all around them were those tiny fish, that they were suspended in a whirling ball of them. Together they moved with the girl and the mermaid through the waters.

"We must get out of here," Syrena said. "This harbor is terrible. So many boats, they push you around like bullies! We need deep water. You are very hurt."

"I can't move," Sophie managed to say.

"I know. Don't talk about it. You are, what is word—destroyed? If you had no magic you would be a dead girl. Is only magic keeping you alive right now. I must get you into deep ocean, for healing."

*   *   *

UNDER THE MERMAID'S arm, both of them held inside the shimmering school—*Like an underwater disco ball,* Sophie thought, dazzled by the swirl of tiny fish—Sophie was carried beneath the harbor. The currents of boats shoved them this way and that, it was like trying to cross a busy street, like running across the parkway where four lanes of traffic whizzed by. The school of fish slowed as a boat passed close, containing them in its wake. All the while Syrena grumbled and cursed the ships, until finally they had crossed from the harbor into the open waters of the Atlantic Ocean.

Finally safe from the party boats that crisscrossed the harbor, Syrena paused, letting Sophie to the ground gently. The disco ball of fish cracked open, releasing them, then hovered close by, a landscape of shining silver. Sophie noticed in all the commotion that she had lost her shoes. Her feet glowed pale and blue beneath the water.

"We have long way to go," the mermaid spoke. "And we swim against the current. I will need all my power, my tail and my arms. So, I will make for you a cocoon. From this." With her luminescent arms the mermaid gathered her hair and shook it wetly at Sophie. Like a sea plant it drifted in the water, swaying in the waves.

The mermaid slid into the heavy sand where Sophie lay like a broken doll, a marionette with cut strings. Never had she been so helpless, splayed on the seafloor like a jellyfish. *No, not a jellyfish,* she thought, watching the globe of a jellyfish pulse by. Jellyfish could move—their glowing balloon bodies were nothing but movement. Sophie was just a bag of bones. Syrena dug into the sand beneath her, and with her strong, flat tail she pushed the girl up the length of her body until Sophie was stretched out on the creature's back.

Syrena's hair, its intricate tangle, settled down over Sophie like a net, binding her to the mermaid's body. Sophie was shocked at the softness of Syrena's skin. How could she be so old and so rugged, and yet her skin soft like a dolphin's? She should be tough as a whale, with barnacles cleaved to her scales, but she wasn't. With her cheek to the mermaid's back, Sophie felt such gratitude for her rescue that she nearly kissed her smooth shoulder, but she couldn't imagine the mermaid would like that, so she didn't.

Syrena pulled her tangles around her like a cape and with deft fingers braided her hair down the front of her body, securing Sophie tightly to her back. The mesh of hair was tight against the girl's face, and she worried briefly about her ability to breathe. Then she remembered she was underwater. Her bones were broken. She was magic, so magic that she could keep herself alive when her body had turned to soup. The thought made her proud, but frightened: sure she was alive, in this lumpy, paralyzed state, but she couldn't begin to imagine how to heal herself. What good was a magic that kept her half dead? *Better than a magic that left you fully dead*, she scolded herself. And she wasn't really half dead. Aside from the fact that she couldn't move and her limbs felt like sandbags, she was doing okay. She could think, her mind was clear, and she was breathing beneath the ocean. Her talisman glowed its faint blue glow, lighting up her mermaid-hair cocoon prettily, illuminating the miniature world of it—tiny fishes darting hither and thither, a hermit crab snared in a snarl poking its spiny head out to look at her.

"You are good," Syrena said plainly, though Sophie knew she meant it as a question.

"I... I think so," Sophie said.

"Yes, very good, I believe." With her hair pulled back from her face, Syrena had a clear view of her surroundings. Beneath her a long-legged crab, spindly as a spider, crept along the sand. Syrena grabbed it and snapped it in half. She tore a leg from the poor creature and dug it back through her hair, poking it in Sophie's face.

"Here," the mermaid commanded. "You eat. Is long swim."

Sophie screwed her face at the food the mermaid was offering. She'd eaten crab before, boiled and dipped in melted butter, but not this deep-sea creature, crusty and raw. "I'm not hungry," she said.

The mermaid scoffed. "Well, you will be," she said. "And when you are hungry enough you will eat mermaid food."

At her words, Sophie suddenly felt a bit frightened about the journey ahead. "This would maybe be a great time to tell me where I'm going. Where you're taking me," she said, slightly more accusingly than she meant to. Sophie didn't want to sound as if the mermaid were kidnapping her, but she did suddenly feel taken hostage—wound into the creature's hair like an insect snared in a web.

"We go to Poland," Syrena said, and in the tough, round sound of her voice Sophie could practically see the place, its pockmarked, cobblestoned streets reflecting the gray sky above. "There is castle on River Vistula, not far from my part of river. It like tourist castle, ya? But castle very big, and there is whole part of building tourists no see. Secret castle inside castle, ya? Boy lives there, your age I think? Tadeusz. I know his great-grandmother very well. His great-grandmother was big hero for Poland. She was a poet."

"A poet?" A poet sounded to Sophie like the opposite of a hero. Heroes went out and rescued people and fought villains. Poets stayed in dusty corners bent over notebooks, writing about trees and giving themselves bad posture. "That's funny," Sophie said. She felt the mermaid buck beneath her sharply; if Sophie hadn't been tied to the mermaid's body with the mermaid's own hair she'd have been flipped right off.

"Funny?" Syrena snapped. "What so funny about that?"

"Just, like, I don't know… a poet being a hero. It's just funny. Because poets are like, you know, they're sort of wimpy."

"'Wimpy'?" The mermaid bucked again, and Sophie was glad that her spine had been pulverized because the mermaid's movement was sharp enough to have snapped it in two. "What is word—'wimpy'?"

"It just means you can't fight that good."

"And you think poet can't fight good?"

"I don't know if *I* think that, exactly, it's more like, the world thinks it. Right? I mean, I've never even met a poet." Sophie was quickly backpedaling away from her original comment. The mermaid was so sensitive!

"Is right you never met poet!" Syrena snapped. "You know poet, you know a poet is a fighter! That place you from, Chelsea? That dump could use a poet! Someone to stand on city square and holler about what a trash place it is! Someone to fight for poor little ungrateful child such as you, get you better education, get you better doctor, ya? What you think poet does?"

"Um, write, right?" Now Sophie was annoyed. "Poets write poems. Little bits of writing that don't make any sense, usually about trees and stuff. Flowers. They're like Hallmark cards."

"What is 'Hallmark card'?"

"They're like, these cards you buy that have a poem written inside them. You get them for Mother's Day, or for a birthday or something."

Sophie could feel Syrena's sigh; the mermaid's body beneath her sagged with it. "Can't even be mad at you," the mermaid said, her voice little more than a mumble. "You too stupid to even be mad at. You live in world without poetry, without poets. You think poet's job to tell your mother happy birthday. You are such a fool you don't even know you are a fool. How can I be mad at such fool? Poet's job to create the world."

Sophie didn't appreciate being called a fool, but it was true she hadn't ever known a poet, so she just kept silent. She hadn't known the mermaid was such a poetry fan. It was just another weird thing about her.

"Tadzio's great-grandmother the poet Krystyna Krahelska. Much famous in Poland. Almost famous as me. In fact, when the city want to make statue of me, they have Krystyna be the model."

"There's a statue of you in Poland?" Sophie asked, and felt Syrena buck again. Sophie understood that every buck was the equivalent of a slap on the head.

"There two statues of me in Poland!" the mermaid roared proudly. "I tell you I am famous, you think I lie, no? What do you know. You girl with no poetry. Well, you will learn in Poland."

"So I'm going to Poland to learn poetry?" Sophie was beyond confused. Her whole life was falling apart, everyone she cared about was in danger, and her grandmother was wicked beyond belief. And she was strapped to a mermaid's back, being stolen away to the old country to learn poetry?

"If I have any say over your education, ya, you learn poetry. And you being brought to Poland for education. You learn about Odmieńce, you learn about Kishka. You learn about yourself. You learn about big story, ya? The whole big story, your story. Pigeons in Chelsea tell you part of story, ya?"

Sophie had a flash of her flock, a body memory of a plump and feathered body settled on her shoulder. "Yes," she said softly.

"And I tell you part story. But there be more. Tadzio know some, he help you."

"Is he magic, too?" Sophie asked. "Is he Odmieńce?"

"No," Syrena said. "He just boy, just human. But he special. I tell you, his great-grandmother big hero."

"So I'm being dragged away from my home, all the way to Poland, to learn about magic from some boy who isn't even magic?" Sophie asked skeptically.

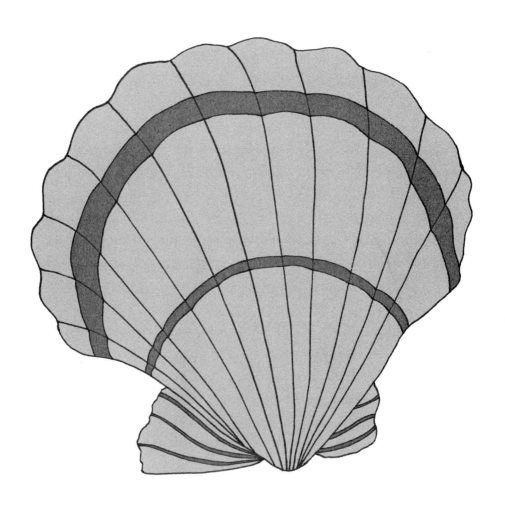

"When you say like that, doesn't sound so good," Syrena agreed. "But I only have my small part to share with you. I have to trust that all the other parts come into place. And you must trust too, Sophie. Whole world depend on it, ya?"

Sophie let the mermaid's last, impossible phrase linger in her mind. *Whole world depend on it.* How could that be? How could the *whole world* depend on her, a girl from Chelsea who barely made it outside her town, not even into Boston, just on the other side of the bridge? Sophie's *whole world* was Heard Street, Bellingham Square. It was Revere Beach a bus ride away, and that was as worldly as it got.

As she felt her anxiety begin to grow, the mermaid spoke again, her voice low and serious. "Plus, there is Invisible. I show it to you, is far out in ocean, but we go there. Invisible have something to do with story, but I don't know what. Not my part to know."

"What is it?" Sophie asked.

"Is like, force, ya?" Sophie could hear the mermaid struggling to explain. "Is like, energy. I wish I was poet, then I could explain better, ya? Invisible is there and not there; something like that takes poet to understand. I don't understand Invisible, maybe you will, with your magic. All I know is Invisible very bad. So bad you can feel it, feel it stronger than you see it. Just wait. We will visit it."

"Well, I can't wait," Sophie said sarcastically. "I'm going to see some bad vibes and then get dumped at a castle so some boy who isn't even magic can teach me something."

"Ya," the mermaid said. "And then you will fight Kishka. And you will win. You must. If you lose, that feeling I showed you when we first met, that terrible badness, that will win. That badness *is* Kishka. So, if I you, I shut up with the smarty-pants—how you say?—bullshit. If I you, I want to learn everything I can from everyone in the world—pigeon, mermaid, boy. If I you, I want to learn every single bit of information I can learn. Because if you lose, we are all—how you say?—screwed."

And with that the mermaid shut up, and so did Sophie. She remembered exactly how it had felt, the first time Syrena had pushed her way into Sophie's heart and showed her who her grandmother really was. So she lay upon the mermaid's back in quiet contemplation, fighting off the fear that threatened to crawl up from her heart and swallow her whole.

Chapter 4

Like a bullet Syrena shot through the waters, the curl and punch of her tail rocking Sophie into a soothing rhythm. The intensity of their conversation faded, and Sophie grew dreamy with the rhythm of the mermaid's motion and the pulsing of the water around her. As they descended, Sophie felt her ears clog and pop. Through the veil of mermaid hair she saw lights in the water, luminescent creatures glowing moonish and blue, or hot pink, bright orange. A strange worm-like thing became snagged in Sophie's net and wriggled blindly across her face. It was fleshy and glowing, with neither a head nor a tail, just color and movement. Sophie was mesmerized. And she understood what the mermaid had promised, that when she got hungry enough she would join her underwater feasting. Though the thought of biting into the alien critter repulsed her, she was drawn to it, too. What would such a thing taste like? It was bright as candy.

Syrena's hand reached behind her and ran down her mane,

searching for food. She found the soft worm and plucked it away from Sophie, popped it in her mouth. After she swallowed with a satisfied sound, she cleared her throat. "So, since I know all about you," Syrena said to her charge, snug on her back like a baby in a papoose, "Now I will tell you all about me. Will help us pass the time to Poland. We have long way to go, ya? And frankly, I do not want to listen to you all the way. Will make me crazy to hear you yammering like human girl for so many days. Will be good for you to be quiet, listen. And be good for you to have something to listen to, so you don't go crazy yourself, in your mind, thinking about all this saving world problem. And who know?" the mermaid asked thoughtfully, "Perhaps something in my story can help you."

"I WAS BORN in a mermaid village," Syrena began. "Just outside the North Sea. Maybe six hundred years ago."

Syrena was born into a village embroiled in a life-or-death debate. At stake was the life of mermaids, and it was the mermaids themselves who were asking the question: with the ocean such a perilous place for them, was it wise to keep creating more mermaids?

There was a feeling, held passionately by many of them, that the sea was no longer a safe place for even the oldest and strongest among them. Of course, life underwater had always been heightened by the fact that at any moment sharks could arrow into the village and leave the water there reddened in their wake. The mermaids had always fortified their homes as best they could, digging great caves beneath the sand or building bunkers from the discarded shells of giant clams and old sea-monster bones. They set traps for the sharks, and some mermaids took up the task of fighting them in combat, armored in seashells, a spear in each hand. What feasts the village had when a mermaid slayed a shark!

To protect their offspring the mermaids constructed castles of foam from their own mouths and nestled their fragile eggs inside. Tucked up in the crook of a sea cave, or hidden in a jumble of rocks, the babies grew from a speck of nothing into the littlest tadpoles, finally clawing out of the soft, watery eggs. They scattered into the sea blindly, instinctively sticking close to rocks, darting into crevices, eating plankton and microbes. The ones who weren't swallowed by fish grew larger. The ones who weren't lassoed by hungry squid grew larger still. Eventually the mermaid babies made their way into the heart of the village, where they were greeted with cheers of joy. These were the hardiest mermaids, the craftiest, the ones with intuition like radar. The grown creatures protected them from seals and sharks and taught them how to be mermaids—how to care for their scales and their hair, how to build caves and spear fish, how to weave nets and make mermaid magic. It was the way they had lived for thousands of years.

But the coming of the people onto the seas changed everything. At first there were only a few, and their boats were humble and so were they. Knowing they were entering another's land, the humans brought gifts for the mermaids, and the mermaids offered their own tokens in return—wreaths woven from seaweed and their own hair, clusters of pearls wrenched from the tight lips of oysters, a perfect fish, wrestled with their own hands.

First there were only a few boats, but then there were many, and the vessels grew larger and larger: no longer a single man rowing the hull of a tree, but a rowdy crew commanding a ship built from an entire forest. They sailed further from their native shores, no longer coming through the nearby channels and straits but cutting across the wide, open ocean.

And the ocean, it appeared, had made them mad. The further they traveled from home, the more troubled the men of the ships seemed to be. They were soiled and dizzy, drunk on poisons they'd made themselves, brewed from potatoes they'd have been better off eating. The men were sickly, and the mermaids felt bad for them, so they pulled themselves onto the rocks and sang.

Song, beneath the ocean, was powerful medicine. The whales knew this—they bathed the hurt and disturbed members of their pods in the vibrations of their voices. As it traveled through the waters, the noise grew in its magic. It was as if the sound directed itself toward the problem, modulated its harmonies to fix it. The songs of the whales soothed illnesses of the body and the spirit, and it was the whales who'd taught the mermaids the power of their own melodies. Mermaids who were torn by shark teeth, or had swum too low into the depths and emerged dark-minded and spooky, were ringed by a floating cotillion of their sisters and bathed in the symphony of their voices, their high squeals and low rumbles, sounds that grew and receded like the sea's own currents. Sound that came together like a school of shimmering fish, sound so bright you could almost see it in the water. Creatures from fathoms away would gather round to listen to the mermaids, gleaning comfort and care from the sounds that bounced off the seafloor. The mermaids' song surrounded them all in a still and sacred moment. The constant hungers of animals who prowled the sea were sated, if only for a moment. Fish who normally swallowed each other whole would look into each other's wide, staring eyes for the first time. The world of the ocean was whole, as if every single creature was a drop of its water.

The mermaids had never sung above the waters, but the sight of the men, so sickly and wild, urged them to try to help with their sounds. And so along the rocks they arranged themselves, and as one they sounded their *zawolanie*—their magic cry.

It was a sound such as the men had never heard. Already crazed from too much drink and time at sea, they raised their faces in despair, sure that their god, a terrible one, had pulled the sky apart with his fist. The sound, to them, was like a tearing, and they looked down, certain they would see their ship itself coming apart around their feet, nails popping from the wood. It was the noise of the end of the world, and it came from the mouths of the fish-women on the rocks, their mouths open as if hungry to eat them all.

The mermaids dove from the rocks as the ship, suddenly freed from the control of its crew, sailed toward them. They saw the sailors' faces, contorted as if in the final throes of death, their grubby hands clamped to their ears. The sound of the mermaids echoed inside their minds; even as the creatures fled beneath the water, their cries seemed to continue. Men slammed their heads into the walls of the ship, trying to shake out the terrible screams; they tore the sails from the mast and wrapped their faces in them. Many, in their agony and confusion, fell from the vessel into the waters.

Beneath the water the mermaid village had been thrown into chaos as well. The mermaids churned about, distraught and alarmed. They had never known their voices to wreak havoc, but without the ocean to soften and carry it, their song's raw power must have been too much. They looked up as the tall boots of sailors, kicking at the sea as if it were a giant beast, punctured the water's surface. The sailors hollered and flailed. Soon, the mermaids knew, the sharks would come for them. Something must be done quickly.

A mermaid swam up to the boots of one sailor and with both hands pulled him beneath the waters. Now his struggle increased, his fists shot out at the mermaids who gathered around him, but the water slowed his motion. A stream of what looked like jellyfish rose upward from his mouth. The mermaids would have to act quickly; he would not last long beneath the waves. Circling the sailor, they began their song anew. The soft ocean waters held the vibrations and brought them to the sailor. And just as moments ago his mind was full of knives, now only tenderness filled him. His body, knotted from months at sea, relaxed. As the waters washed from him the grime of his time at sea, the mermaids' song cleaned his head and his heart.

When it seemed he was healed, the one who still held his boots gave her tail a powerful kick and pushed him up above the waters. He broke the surface like a boy reborn—and really, he was just a boy. No longer aged by the harshness of a sailor's life, the mermaids could see that he was not much older than a human child.

The mermaids rose behind the boy and swam to the rocks, where more sailors did strange dances of pain. The first mermaid to arrive was received with a boot in the face.

"Witches!" the sailor howled. The mermaids paddled back quickly, but the men struck out, catching some in the face and head with their boots and fists. More shocked than hurt, they scattered beneath the waters.

"They cured me!" the boy they had healed shouted to the men on the deck of the ship, a ship that had been gouged by the rocks, a ship that was crumbling and sinking. The boy saw what his crew had busied themselves with even if the mermaids did not, and he waved his hands, frantic, above the waters.

"They are peaceful!" the boy cried. "They cured my mind—I hear the screams no more!"

"The screams are theirs!" shouted his captain. "They've sunk us! Sea witches! They have bewitched you, young lad, you've been deviled!" Sparks shot from the captain's hand as he brought his flaming fist to the rope of the cannon.

The mermaids had never seen a cannon before.

*　*　*

AS THEY TRAVELED, time passed in a blur for Sophie, bundled like a baby on the mermaid's back with visions of mermaids and sailors flitting through her mind like dreams. When Syrena ended her tale and finally stopped swimming, there was only the epic quiet of the ocean and the surges of currents washing over them—warm water, then cold, then colder, then a rush of warm again. They were so deep it was like being nowhere. *Outer space,* Sophie thought hazily, weightless in the dark water. She felt like an astronaut of sorts. When the mermaid undid the tangles of hair that cocooned her, Sophie floated down onto the sandy ocean floor, thinking, *This is another planet entirely.*

When she looked up toward the sky, Sophie expected to see nothing, a void, in this place where the sun had never shone. But what she saw in the darkness was a great wall, a darkness upon the darkness that rose high above them. Sophie's eyes adjusted to the dim glow of her sea-glass talisman, the light fighting against the extinguishing weight and blackness of the depths.

It looked like a mountain range that rose up as far as she could see and extended all the way to the edges of her vision. But it made Sophie think of the wall inside her, that dark fortress Angel taught her to pull up around her heart so that no one—not good-hearted Angel or evil-hearted Kishka—could get inside, so Sophie decided to regard the epic strength and darkness rising before her as a safe space, not a sinister one. A place for them to rest.

"Talk about the *middle of nowhere!*" Sophie said aloud and started to giggle, a bit overwhelmed. Even if she was part *znakharka,* Polish witch, she was still part teenage girl, and she was a human girl at the bottom of the sea, looking up at the biggest mountain the earth had ever kicked up. As her eyes continued to adjust, Sophie could spot thin streaks of brightness at its black peak, orange flares that shone and vanished. Were her eyes playing tricks?

"Can you see?" Syrena asked, swirling down to the floor beside her. The mermaid stretched, raising her arms high above her head and unfurling her giant tail onto the sand. She pointed toward the mountaintop with her long, pale finger, blue in the glow of their talismans. Syrena's sea glass sat upon her bare chest, a starfish trapped in its center like a bug in amber. Sophie's, sitting on her grubby t-shirt, held a seashell. The blue light shone up to their faces, and their eyes met: Sophie's wide with wonder, the mermaid's ageless, ancient, with their own luminescence.

"It is the earth birthing itself," Syrena said. "Special place. The mountain—how you say it?—barfing out hot liquid earth, water-fire."

"It's called lava," Sophie said.

Syrena rolled her eyes, a faint strobe in the darkness. "Yes, lava. Don't be show-off. The lava barf is cooled and hard and becomes the earth. This is where everything happens. Powerful place. Good place to fix you."

They lay there, watching the orange tongues lapping at the peak as if they were fireworks in the sky. A fire in the sea. Here and there, great explosions of what looked like black smoke shot from cracks in the endless crags.

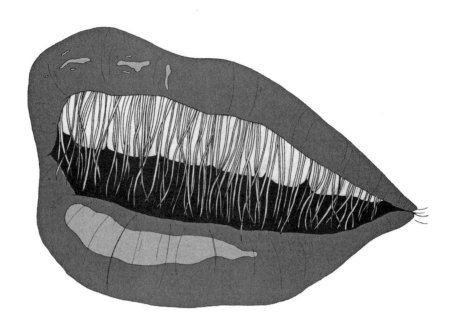

"Just water," Syrena said. "Much minerals in it, make it dark. Very rich water, very healthy for us."

Beneath them the ocean floor trembled, a daisy chain of earthquakes as the mountain did its eternal work creating more of the planet. Syrena leaned into Sophie and offered a lock of her hair. "Hungry yet?" the mermaid smiled. For thousands of miles, her hair had acted like a net, a trawler capturing algae and plankton, small shrimp and fishes. Syrena grabbed a thick lock of it. It was messy and weird, yet the dark tangle Syrena had dangled in front of Sophie's nose smelled oddly delicious. Sophie's belly rumbled. How long had it been since she had eaten? How long *had* she traveled on the mermaid's back? Sophie opened her mouth to the tangle, and it was like eating a great stew. Tastes she'd never known, green tastes and blue tastes, deep and oceanic. Everything salty and briny and delicious. Syrena bowed her head to the girl and Sophie nibbled right up to the roots.

"Okay!" the mermaid snapped, slapping away Sophie's hands. "I am not buffet! This is *me*." She shook the lock, cleaned of algae and the edible dust of the sea, at Sophie. "You pull my hair, it hurts."

"Sorry," Sophie burped.

"How is it you feel?" Syrena asked. "Still you can't move?"

Sophie nodded her head. "Only my head." She paused, and then spoke out loud a thought that had been haunting her. "Syrena, is there something wrong... with my magic?" She swallowed nervously. "Shouldn't I be able to fix myself?"

"Even if you half Odmieńce, you can't do everything. Nothing can. Everything need help, everyone. I will help you. And this place, it will help you." Syrena scooped a palmful of mud from the ocean floor and gazed at it by the light of their talisman. It sparkled with phosphorescence like neon, and seemed to wriggle with the movement of things too small to see. Sophie watched in horror as the mermaid tossed the glob of mud into her mouth. A fringy bristle she had never before noticed hung like a broom over Syrena's teeth, and she sucked at the mud, ingesting the plankton and minerals while the brush caught the sand. With a very unladylike noise, the mermaid blew the mud from the bristles, and then the bristles disappeared.

Syrena smiled at the girl, her own teeth pearly as abalone shell. "What?" she demanded. "You never see retractable baleen before? You lie there with your mouth open, you will wish you had some too!"

Indeed, Sophie's mouth was a bit muddy from hanging open in shock. She tried to spit it out, but it crunched in her teeth. "Retractable baleen?"

"Like whale," Syrena shrugged. "But it comes and goes. See?" The mermaid opened her mouth wide, and above her teeth Sophie spied not gums but bits of brush. With a flex the baleen came down, a curtain that allowed the good stuff to pass into the mermaid's mouth but filtered sand and grit. The baleen rose, and Syrena spoke.

"Quite handy," she said.

"Are you part whale?" Sophie asked, and Syrena shrugged.

"Perhaps. Like you are part monkey. But we are part human, too, so perhaps mermaids part monkey as well."

"And people are part whale?"

Syrena scoffed, a bubble of air shooting out from her nose. "You wish."

"Syrena, where *are* we?"

"Mid-Atlantic Ridge, is called by you people. We stay here a bit."

Syrena gathered Sophie in her arms and let the muscle of her tail propel them up the side of the mountain. *Like flying*, Sophie thought, passing over fissures and valleys rising toward the lakes of lava that bubbled at the top. Sophie could see great molten globs of it crawling from the mountain's lip and sliding down, cooling into rock. Baby earth.

They settled into the soft earth of a high crevice below the range of the hottest lava. The ridge of rock was solid and the water there was warm, strikingly so after the frigid depths of the Atlantic. Sophie felt a tingling as sensation returned to her skin. She hadn't even realized she had been so cold.

"Oh this is so nice," Sophie murmured, finding herself lying on a vent that bubbled soothing hot water all over her. "Like a spa." Sophie had never been to a spa, but she had seen pictures in magazines of women looking impossibly relaxed, with mud on their faces and slices of cucumber on their eyes, soaking in a tub. And Sophie sure did have mud on her face—both she and Syrena were streaked with it.

"Are you comfortable, Sophie?" Syrena asked.

"Mmmm-hmmmm," the girl mumbled.

"Very good. Then I will sing to you. Heal you, like my kind have done for generations."

Hovering over Sophie, with her talisman floating down until it bumped gently into Sophie's own, Syrena began her song. It ricocheted off the mountain range, its power multiplying with echoes. It engulfed Sophie as completely as the water, becoming one with the water and soaking into the girl, streaming into her ears, her nose, her mouth. *Heaven*, Sophie thought. *This must be what heaven is.* The sound moved into her bones and made them whole again, turned them to song. Sophie was the song, the song was she and she was everything. What a gift it was, the mermaid's harmony. Sophie had thought that a mermaid's song was something that washed over you; now she understood it was something you *became*. Sophie was Syrena's song—and Sophie was healed.

"Oh!" Sophie cried when the last bit of echo had faded into the darkness. She flung her arms up around the mermaid's neck, buried her face in her hair, the source of her sustenance. It was as if Syrena were the ocean itself, and everything it had to give.

"Okay, okay, okay, now now," Syrena peeled her charge off of her. "Not too fast, not too fast, okay? Your bones are whole, but they weak like baleen, okay?" The mermaid brought the brush back down across her teeth and flicked them with an opal fingernail. "They still weak. You will lie here and eat the minerals in the water, you will soak in the salt and I will sing and we will talk. *Dobrze?*"

"Dobrze," Sophie agreed, effortlessly translating and speaking the mermaid's Polish. As she reclined upon the vent, Sophie became aware of the nutrients in the hot water, microscopic shrimps and algae, and it was as if she were lounging in a giant pot of stew. She drank from it sloppily, without baleen to strain the crunchy bits of cooled lava. Soon she began to enjoy the bite of the lava, the smash of glass and crystal beneath her teeth.

"Is good for you, too," the mermaid nodded approvingly. "You have the intuition. Your body tell you what it wants. Lava is good medicine—iron, calcium." She plucked a porous black crumb from the earth beneath her and popped it in her mouth, sucking on it like a candy. The molten lava above them glowing like candlelight, the two fell into a soft and salty slumber.

Chapter 5

Though Syrena's mother, whoever she might be—mermaids never knew what batch of eggs they'd hatched from, since they were raised and nurtured by the entire village—had had the run of the ocean for all her long life, Syrena was born into a world that was struggling with the idea of boundaries. Borders. For the first time there were places the mermaids could not go. Of course they'd learned to avoid the lairs of sharks and other unfriendly beasts, but this was different. As the humans above them carved out trade routes, highways that took them right into mermaid territory, so the mermaids' landscape shrank, carved by the wake of the great boats streaming above them, strange waves that came not from the moon but from the cleaving of the waters by those terrible vessels.

And terrible they were. With each passing season they had grown more majestic, their sails now big as clouds, their hulls built with the wood of a whole forest. No longer just a single cannon but a row of them edged each boat's decks. With great caution the mermaids snuck above the waves and spied the great ships fearfully. By now they understood that the humans fought with one another frequently, and that the cannons were there for them to destroy each other, not the sea creatures. But the mermaids also knew that the humans would be as quick to fire at them, should any of them show their faces.

As the ships sailed past the edge of the mermaid village, their captains would order themselves tied tightly to their post with lengths of rope, lest the mermaids begin singing and drive them mad. The rest of the crews lingered by the cannons, itching to fire. And fixed to the bows of these boats were statues carved of wood in the image of the most beautiful mermaids, hair streaming and breasts perky, a long fishtail of many colors undulating beneath them. The mermaids were enchanted and baffled by these likenesses. Why, if the sailors meant them harm, would they decorate their precious ships with their image? It infuriated the elders, who took it as foolish disrespect, and they suggested that the villagers crawl upon the rocks and sing the ships to their doom. How dare they use the magic mermaid image to appease the sea, as if the mermaids were *not* the sea?

Many other mermaids agreed, and for a time a secret cadre of them would slip above the waves to torment the sailors who would create such things. In return, cannon fire crumbled the rocks they loved to lie upon to sun, and ships were torn into by the broken rocks and sunk below the surface. Then the mermaids, old and young alike, were left with the spectacle of these ruined vessels crashed down in the middle of their village, heaped with drowned sailors.

The tenderest of them wept at the tragedy, and even the hardest could see how wrong it was to bring such destruction, whether to mermaids or to men. So the mermaids packed up their shells and spears, their instruments and hair combs, the costumes they wore for dancing and the tools they made for building. Heaping their things onto giant clamshells, they wove ropes from weeds and hair and lashed them to the shells, passing the reins to a pod of dolphins who had offered to help. With squeals of pleasure, the dolphins tugged the clam-sleighs through the waters, for dolphins see even the most tedious task as play; everything makes them happy. The mermaids swam alongside them, scanning for a home deep enough to elude the humans, yet not *too* deep. Living in the very depths of the ocean is not healthy; the darkness and pressure weigh heavily on the mermaid mind and bring about a great and creepy depression.

Into the North Sea swam the mermaids, eventually coming upon a raised bed littered with boulders and rocks, the debris left behind by a long-ago glacier. "Oh!" The most enthusiastic among them clapped their hands and beat their tails, imagining what they could build from such raw materials. Forts and caves, crooks to lounge in, jumbles to hide the ephemeral castles of mermaid foam that held the eggs of their offspring.

"It's too high," grumbled the elders.

"And so the ships will avoid it," another countered.

"It is made for us!" cried most of them. "A gift of the sea!"

Finally, it was decided: the mermaids would claim as their home the sprawling Dogger Bank, as the humans called it, but as a precaution against ships and their blood-hungry humans they would dig a great valley of trenches nearby, a place for them to flee should trouble come to the village.

A new chapter of industry began for this pod of mermaids. The tougher among them, the ones who enjoyed wrestling sharks and getting into tangles with giant squids, swam out to deeper sea, and with shovels fashioned from shell and bone they began to dig deep furrows into the ocean floor. Flipping piles of mud from their tails, they watched the walls of earth rise around them as they dug deeper and deeper.

"How do you feel?" the mermaids would inquire of one another on their lunch and snack breaks. Munching on mackerel and cod, cracking open shellfish with their sharpened canines, they considered the question.

"Quite well," one might murmur, "but I can feel a sort of flat doom coming on like a sneeze."

"Me as well," another mermaid would nod. And so after they fed, they pushed silt and mud from the banks, raising the trenches to a happier level.

"This is perfect!" a worker affirmed at last, wriggling around in the lush, wet mud, sifting the nutrients in the silt through her baleen happily. "This will be a great place to hide if we must!"

It also proved to be a great place for the mermaids to find food.

The humans had begun to hang nets from their boats, allowing them to drag in the wake of their vessels, scooping up a bounty of creatures. But as they passed over the trenches their nets would catch and pull, sticking in the ditches until the sailors were forced to cut them loose. The mermaids would find wonderful bundles of fish waiting for them, as if dropped by a benevolent sea goddess. "Devil's Hole," the fishermen came to call it, and worked to avoid the mermaids' hiding place. But such a wide spot was hard to avoid, and so it became a regular mermaid task to journey out to the trenches and gather up what the fishermen had dropped.

LIKE A HUMAN child, Syrena had no memory of her life as a tadpole, no idea how she had escaped being gobbled up by a mackerel or trapped in the mouth of a clam. She may have been a wily baby, or she may have only been lucky. All she knew is she made it to the village, led by that mysterious instinct that had always led baby mermaids to their village.

Syrena's first clear recollection was of a village meeting during which the passions of the mermaids ran high enough that it seemed they began to produce their own currents and raise the water's temperature. The issue was whether or not the mermaids would stop laying their eggs and creating more mermaids.

"Preposterous!" many cried. Laying eggs was simply what mermaids *did*, like singing and building villages, like riding dolphins and shedding their tarnished scales for the beautiful, gleaming ones beneath.

"How can we *stop* laying our eggs?" one mermaid asked, baffled. It was like asking their gills to stop filtering oxygen from the waters, asking their hearts to stop beating, their hair to stop growing.

"We will leave them to the sea," an elder spoke grimly.

There was a gasp from the shocked, and stoic nodding and mumbles from those who believed they must freeze the growth of their village.

One of the warrior mermaids rose up from the clamshell on which she'd lounged. "I have traveled, and I have seen many things and spoken to many other mermaids," she began. She was tough and fearsome, with great scars lacing her tail. Her hair was wound around her head and knotted like a turban, and her eyes flashed. A jagged shell dagger topped with a sea-monster fang was bound to her muscled arm with shark leather. The village grew silent with respect, for this mermaid had saved many of them from the attacks of sea beasts. She had helped to build the structure they were gathered under, she had helped to dig the trenches and harvested the fish, and she had ventured far into the sea, even during this treacherous time, to monitor the travels of the humans, their movements across the oceans.

"I have swum south and seen the most terrible of ships," she continued. "They are great floating villages, filled with people the humans have stolen. They take their own kind from their homelands and shackle them in the bowels of these ships and sail them across our oceans, far away from their homes. The ships are full of misery and disease. They trade their own kind the way we trade pearls or bone. They beat and torture them and make them work like animals."

"Their own kind?" the mermaids repeated, looking about, confused. "Other humans? You are certain?"

"Men and women, even children. Chained to the boats as if they were cannons, not living creatures."

"If they do such things to one another, what would they do to us?" an elder exclaimed, and the warrior turned to address her.

"I can tell you," she said. "In the east, the fishermen are hunting our sisters like whales. For food."

"Food!"

"They think they can eat our magic," she said. "In the south, the mermaids who try to free the captured humans have been slaughtered, their tails nailed to the ships as a warning."

At this news, the tenderest among them began to cry, while the toughest grew even harder against the humans.

"Closest to us, in the west, mermaids have been captured and put to terrible purpose. The men try to keep us as wives—"

"Out of the water?"

"Yes, on the land. Kept in a house, like a human wife. Or kept in a filthy tank, shown at fairs like beasts."

The mermaids' heads and hearts spun with confusion and despair. "But we are a nation!" cried one elder. "How dare they not reckon with us!"

"Maid, they do not reckon with one another," the warrior said softly, at last allowing a glimmer of her own sadness to show. "They will not reckon with us. We must prepare. They come deeper and deeper into our waters."

Syrena was curled on the lap of the mermaid who had first claimed her when she swam into the village, the one who had cared for her the most. She wrapped Syrena in her great, strong braids, binding the baby to her chest. Syrena's chubby tail wiggled in the water and her fist clutched and rattled the seedpod she kept as a toy. The older mermaid hugged baby Syrena tightly and cried into her soft hair. Only one other baby had swum into the village since Syrena had appeared nearly a year ago—her sister, Griet. She was being bounced on the tail of another tearful mermaid close by, teething her new canines on a thick chunk of the mermaid's hair. The two baby mermaids, Syrena and Griet, had beaten the odds and made it to the village. And as the village cast its vote, so it was decided that no more would.

"Only for a time," the elders said, hoping to take the edge off the younger mermaids' sadness.

"Only for a time," the mermaids all repeated to one another, their voices strained with desperate hope.

"Only for a time," they consoled themselves as they set their eggs adrift in the sea, turning their backs to the schools of fish gathered for a feeding frenzy. They swallowed the foam meant to protect their creations, choking on its bitter taste.

Chapter 6

When Sophie awoke, the first thing she thought was, *I can move!* She kicked her legs out beneath her and brought her arms up in a long, delicious stretch. Oh, it felt so *good* to have a body! How strange had been these past days when she'd been reduced to a sort of amoeba, a brain inside a shell—like a clam, she thought, but even clams could move. Cuddled into the crook of Syrena's great tail, Sophie grew excited at the thought of swimming alongside the mermaid. There, at the bottom of the sea, it was easy to forget a world existed above them, but it did. And Sophie would see it. *Poland.* What would it be like? She found herself yearning to see the sun again. She could barely remember what it felt like to stand beneath its yellowy glow.

Bringing her hands to her face to wipe away the mud and bits of mermaid scale stuck to her cheeks from using Syrena's tail as a pillow, Sophie started. Her hands had been clenched into fists since the great wave had pounded her, and now, as she spread her fingers, she found

tucked inside her palm a bit of softness, iridescent in the glow of her talisman. A feather.

Livia.

Sophie remembered the moments before her grandmother summoned the waters, when she'd plucked from the sky above her *Livia*, graceful and sweet-hearted, the pigeon whose love was so pure and true Sophie could still feel it inside her—the bird's love for her crotchety husband and their beautiful children, her love for the humans who had lost their way and fallen into cruelty, her love for Sophie, the girl the pigeons had spoken of for so long, anticipating her coming. Livia had helped her and Livia had loved her. And it was because of Sophie that Livia was dead. Sophie's tears squeezed from her eyes and merged with the sea; she was her own sad creek, sending trickles of salt into the ocean.

It was this way that Syrena found her, crumbled into a wet heap of a girl, Livia's feather held tight in her hand. Syrena knew at once what was paining Sophie. She'd known that once Sophie regained her faculties, great grief was awaiting her. So Syrena came to her, wrapped her tail around the girl and stroked her hair with her long, cool fingers.

"What will Arthur do?" Sophie cried to the mermaid. Arthur with his hobbled feet, wounded from the chemicals people left out to try to rid the streets of pigeons. How Arthur had relied on Livia for her strength and humor and love. It was Livia's brightness that kept cranky Arthur from sliding too deeply into hurt and anger. What would he become without her?

"Arthur will get by without her," the mermaid said resolutely. She knew the girl might find her cold, but there was nothing to be done about it. Lives passed so quickly on land that the creatures who dwelled there could never become accustomed to death. In the oceans, life spanned millennia, and so thousands of deaths are witnessed and one learned to accept it. Syrena had lived for many years and had witnessed many wars and many atrocities in the sea and on the banks of her river, and she knew that she accepted Arthur's plight in a way Sophie could not. She could feel the girl's heart rage against it. Syrena could not tell if this feeling of humans was a sweet thing or an annoyance. They were like small children in this way, forever confused by the ways of life, of death's inherent part in it. But of course it was sweet. The mermaid could feel the pounding of love behind the girl's tears.

So Syrena let Sophie cry, but after a time the mermaid knew they must move on. She saluted the brave life of the dead bird, and the sorrow of the family she had left behind. And then it was time to go. They were still in the middle of the Atlantic; they had a long way to travel.

"I will teach you some swimming tricks now." Syrena gave the girl a last pat and pulled back her tail. "You are ready."

Sophie, still mourning for Livia and her flock, suddenly bristled at the way the mermaid always spoke her questions as statements. "It's not 'You are ready,'" she corrected sharply. "It's 'Are you ready?' or 'You are ready?'"

"As I said," Syrena replied. "You are ready. Don't be dumb."

"'You are *ready*?'" Sophie stressed through gritted teeth, bringing her voice up at the end. "You *ask*. Otherwise it's rude." She pulled at the stringy tendrils hanging from the bottom of her cutoff shorts, annoyed.

"What is—rude? When I speak to you plain and direct like mermaid speak? You can't handle it? I say too bad for you," Syrena snorted, tiny bubbles flaring from her nose. "Humans have hardly any life and spend most of it crying. If worst thing to happen to you today is mermaid rudeness, I think good day for you, ya? Now, come. We swim. You are ready."

"Since you are *asking*, no, I am *not* ready," Sophie said, barely containing the tears building hotly again behind her eyes. "I'm trying to deal with the fact that someone I love is *dead*, and other people I love are in pain and danger, and it's all *my fault!*" The sob burst forth, a shimmer in the water around Sophie's face. She glared at the mermaid as if she were a monster.

Syrena shrugged, feeling the girl's thoughts. "Well, I am what you call *monster*," she allowed. "More or less. I know is sad Livia gone. More reason we swim now. Must fight Kishka, yes? Avenge your friend? You don't fight Kishka with crying."

Syrena plucked the feather from Sophie's hand, and before the girl could protest she was at work deftly braiding it into Sophie's long, messy hair. "You on your way to becoming real mermaid," she said with something like tenderness. "So much tangle in your hair!"

The touch of the mermaid's fingers could not help but calm Sophie down. The stroke and scratch of Syrena's nails as she wove locks around Livia's feather soothed her. She closed her eyes, and her tears came slower. Steady, but slower. The rush of memory was almost too much. Dr. Chen—how she loved her birds! How she had woven the lovely flute into Livia's tails with affection and care. Angel, who had been on the banks of the creek as the rogue wave descended. Her mother, all alone without Sophie's protection. Even Ella, left to a different sort of peril, her own compulsions and the compulsions of the boys she now spent her time with. How could Sophie help them—how could she help anyone, a million miles beneath the ocean, in the earth's darkest place?

"I think we've made a mistake," she said to the mermaid. "What are we doing here? We've got to go back! We've got to help everyone! Why did we leave Chelsea?" Sophie was wracked with urgency and homesickness.

"You must trust, Sophie," Syrena said, patting her hair into place.

The feather was braided so that it hung along the girl's cheek, brushing it gently. Sophie reached out and touched it, pulling it before her eyes. Even in the darkness, the rainbow sheen of Livia's feather glinted, iridescent.

"Thanks," Sophie said softly.

"Is true we must get out of here," Syrena said briskly. "So—you are ready now."

"'*Are* you ready now?'" Sophie corrected. "And yes," she sighed. "I am."

*   *   *

"MORE ELEGANT!" SYRENA hollered to Sophie, watching her make her way through the waters. The girl's arms shot out in front of her, grasping at the water and pushing it jerkily behind her. Her body bucked awkwardly; she looked like a frog, only less elegant. And Syrena didn't find frogs very elegant to begin with.

The real problem was Sophie's legs. They bowed and kicked and flailed. They propelled the girl forward—Sophie *was* swimming—but to Syrena it looked like a complete disaster. In the time it took for Sophie to move twenty feet, Syrena could have been a mile into the depths.

"Like this," Syrena commanded. She stretched the length of her body, uncurling her tail, letting it undulate gently in the water. She laid her arms before her, demonstrating good, elegant swimming posture. She turned her head to Sophie. "You see? Now, you."

Sophie kicked her legs behind her and stretched her arms out. It was a pose she could not hold. Her body would begin to fall this way or that, sinking and bobbing. She tried again, working to approximate the delicate ripple of the mermaid's tail with her own bony legs. She tried to undulate but only jerked as if in the throes of a seizure.

"Okay, okay, very well, keep trying."

For a moment Sophie almost had it, slinking in an underwater full-body belly dance. But immediately she lost the rhythm and sunk back down in a tangle of arms and legs.

"Syrena, I'm not a mermaid," Sophie complained. "I don't have a tail. I can't just, you know, lounge around the water like you do. I'm a *person*. I have to swim or I just sink, you know?" Her hand rose up and gently stroked the pigeon feather wound into her hair. How swiftly this had become a little habit of comfort, but Sophie needed a lot of comfort. Even with a mermaid for a coach, she was failing her swim test.

"I had not thought of this problem," Syrena admitted. "I just think—you swim. How you say—big deal? Is no big deal. You breathe, you eat, you swim." Syrena felt almost embarrassed at how mermaid-centric her assumptions had been. She had spent time here and there with humans, but never in her territory, beneath the waters. Of course they could not manage below the waves as she could.

"Try walking, okay?" Sophie grumbled. "I could totally outwalk you on any piece of land on this earth. I bet you can't even walk at *all*. I bet you have to, like, crawl."

"Is true," the mermaid admitted. "I can not walk even a small bit."

"At least I can swim a small bit," Sophie said proudly.

"Okay, fine, you win."

"Have you ever even *been* on earth?" Sophie asked the mermaid, curious. "On the land?"

Syrena nodded. "Once, very long time ago. I was young, perhaps your age. Was very terrible."

"What happened?"

Syrena sighed. "Here," she said, and held out her tail to the girl. "You hold on, I pull you."

And they headed off like that in the direction of the North Sea. At first it was fun, but as Syrena gained velocity, Sophie started to panic. She might as well have been a fish caught in the mermaid's hair or a hermit crab stowed away in the crook of her hip fins, for Syrena pumped her tail powerfully, beating against the waters as she rocketed against the current, with no thought about the teenager hanging on to her tail for dear life.

Clasping the mermaid's dense, slippery tail with her hands wouldn't work, so Sophie wrapped her arms around the end in a desperate hug. With the force of the waters pulling at her and the relentless twisting of the mermaid's movements threatening to shake her off, Sophie's body shook like a flag in a hurricane. She thought of fake cowgirls on mechanical bulls, how they got flung off, their butts on the ground. Where would Sophie land if Syrena flicked her off her tail? And would the mermaid even know she was gone?

"Syrenaaaaaaaaaaa!" Sophie hollered. But her mouth filled with water as her cry bubbled out, lost in their wild wake as they cut through the ocean. Could she risk lifting a hand off the tail, to give the mermaid a smack? Even loosening her grip destabilized her. She would go spinning off into the water, a one-girl whirlpool. There was only one way to get the mermaid's attention. Sophie bit Syrena's tail.

Her first try, just a nibble, didn't even register. The mermaid's scales were tough, thick, and they were slick like the rest of her skin but not nearly as soft as the skin of her upper body. So Sophie went in harder the next time, channeling a shark. And it worked. With an underwater shriek, the mermaid bucked and slammed her tail, and Sophie's curiosity about what would happen to her if she flew off her ride was satisfied. She was flipped, head over heels, high into the water above their heads—catapulted, as if shot from a cannon. In the dark waters she couldn't tell which way was up and she flailed, trying to right herself. The rapid ascent hurt, shooting cramps through her chest and making her ears pop like gunshot.

Sophie groped blindly at the ocean around her until she noticed, coming from above, the faintest blue light growing stronger. It was the mermaid, appearing not from above but below. With a yank of the girl's arms, Syrena straightened Sophie in the waters, then hung there, glaring at her. The girl was dizzy from her tumbling, her ears clogged and popping. The ocean around them was cloudy with the black curls of water spouting from vents in the floor beneath them.

"What that about?" Syrena demanded. "You hungry? Here—" she shot her hand out into the dark and snagged a baby octopus, thrust the squirm of it at Sophie. "Eat this. Don't eat mermaid!"

"I wasn't *eating* you, Syrena!" Sophie accepted the small octopus and let its tentacles twine her fingers. "I was trying to get your attention! I can't hold on to your tail like that. We need to do something else." The octopus half climbed, half swam, in its mysterious octopus way, up Sophie's arm.

"You very much baby," Syrena observed. "I know this be tough for spoiled human girl from the land. To bring you into *Maumarr*."

"To bring me where?" Sophie asked, confused.

"Maumarr," the mermaid repeated. Her voice in the first part of the word sounded low and sonic, like a whale, then ending in what sounded like a growl. "This place is Maumarr. Mermaid word for the sea."

"Maoooooo," Sophie began awkwardly, and Syrena shushed her.

"Don't," she said. "Human girl cannot make mermaid sound, cannot speak mermaid language. I use your words for things, so you understand. But mermaids have our own words, you know. Older words than your human words. We be down here longer, we know it all forever. Humans not understand life here. Is cold, and hard. You must be strong." The mermaid shook her head, remembering that she was annoyed with the girl for biting her tail, and even for riding along on her body in the first place. "What am I, a bus?"

"Well, I don't know," Sophie tried not to whine, not to be "very much baby." The octopus had drifted up her neck, tickling as it moved into the salty tangle of her hair. "You really can't carry me?" she asked the mermaid. "Am I too heavy?"

"No, Syrena sighed. "Very light. Tell truth, can't feel you at all. Is just principle. I am not donkey. I was told—when I come for you—that you are magic girl, and I think magic girl can swim."

The octopus had settled itself on the top of Sophie's head, sort of off to the side like a little hat. It nibbled some crab larvae from her hair, its many legs burrowing into Sophie's snarls. She reached up and gingerly stroked the tiny beast the way she had taken to stroking Livia's feather, wound in her curls. Her hair was becoming a real catchall.

Syrena sighed deeply, releasing a chain of shimmering bubbles in the water. "Okay," she thought out loud. "You are part girl, which cannot swim like mermaid. You don't have this," Syrena stretched the marvel of her tail before them, gathered it into her arms, petting herself. Frowning, she picked at some scaly bits that hung from her long appendage. "I am mess," she said grimly. "When all is over, I get my tail fixed. Anyway—girl part cannot swim with girl body, ya. But Odmieńce has magic." The mermaid's flashing eyes lit upon Sophie. "Do not try to swim like girl. Swim like Odmieńce!"

Sophie gathered herself in the water. Swim like Odmieńce? She tried to feel powerful. She would charge powerfully forward, like a super-hero bursting into the air! She counted to three in her head and lunged forward sloppily, tripping over her feet. She sunk into a hot cloud and emerged with her face sooty from minerals. It was even more bum-bling than when she was simply trying to swim. Syrena cringed and covered her face with the tip of her tail.

Gritting her teeth, bits of sand and minerals crunching beneath, Sophie hurled herself through the water again and again. But each time she just flailed, lacking even the grace of slapstick. She kicked the underwater geysers and muddied the waters. Syrena grew weary. It did not take long; patience was not one of the mermaid's magics.

"Listen, I told you are big special! I not abandon my river to the *Boginki* unless you real big deal! But this? This, how you say—bullshit!" Syrena's hands were balled into fists, planted on her hips above her little fins. "You want to go against Kishka? Kishka command the water into a fist to pummel us! You can't even swim through it!"

Sophie remembered her terror as the creek rose up at her grand-mother's command. What she saw as she was punched into the sky—her grandmother's many faces reflected in the water as if in a million shards of glass. Kishka did not move through the water, she made the water move. She was Odmieńce, 100 percent. But Sophie was only half. And was it even half? It's not like she'd been tested at some sort of Magic Lab. Who knew—maybe her Odmieńce gene was weak. Maybe there had been a rotten mistake. She looked glumly at her impatient tutor.

"You command the waters," Syrena said flatly. "Or I summon a dolphin to bring you back to creek in Chelsea. I'll be done with you."

Sophie gazed out into the water. It was like looking into a dark sky—grayness all around, monsoon clouds erupting from the floor. She knew there were millions of molecules here, but it looked like nothing. Darkness. She felt her magic pouch still tied to her belt loops, hanging soggy in the water. What was even inside it now? Mud? She poked and squeezed it, but was not called to it. She dropped it, and it floated limply beside her.

While she waited, Syrena plucked a piece of shell from her hair and busied herself filing her opalescent fingernails into wicked points. She curled her lips and brought down her baleen, coated in debris from the geyser. With a huff she blew it all back into the ocean.

Sophie turned away from her. She didn't want to waste her time hating the mermaid. It wouldn't help her out of this problem, this terrible problem—thousands of miles beneath the sea, far from any land, and barely able to swim. She bit down her rising panic. She closed her eyes and floated. She breathed in and out slowly, slowly, letting the water hold her. And it did, it did hold her. She was suspended ever so lightly above the vents in the ocean floor, the hot clouds billowing around her.

What was holding her, exactly? What was water? It moved at the command of the moon, coming in strong and pulling back. It moved at the command of her grandmother, gathering itself, working against nature. Was Kishka the ocean itself? Had they swum deeper and deeper to escape something that was now all around them, something endless just waiting to strike them again? Would the sea suddenly hurl them into the sky, or would it wrap around their throats like an ocean-sized anaconda? What was this water they moved through?

"Syrena, is the water... could it be Kishka? Could she turn into the whole ocean? Is the ocean on her side?"

The mermaid looked at Sophie evenly and shook her head. "Ocean my home always. Ocean is ocean. Is water, is element. Basic. Like air, like fire and the earth, the lava and sand and dirt. Elements are neutral. If you have magic to work them, you make them good or evil, like puppets."

Sophie remembered the fist-shaped wave punching up from the water. She remembered the flash of her grandmother in her beastly bird formation, reflected in every drop of the creek. How powerful was Kishka, able to summon and control nature itself: perhaps she was nature, an unknown force of it. But Sophie was Kishka's granddaughter. She might not be able to summon the waters and make them box for her, but surely she could figure out how to swim.

Sophie calmed herself and grew quiet. She began to truly feel the water, alive all around her. Though she felt stillness in its embrace, she became aware of its motion, its constant shifting, the way it perpetually morphed and flowed over her body. The waters accommodated her, filling the space around her as she bobbed and floated. Its motion was never ending; its thought—*thought?*—ancient and eternal.

The waters, Sophie suddenly understood, were *alive*. She understood it deep in her body, half girl, half Odmieńce, a body made up of so much water—indeed, *most* of her body was water, and Sophie started to feel the communication happening. Her body's water in conversation with the ocean around her, like the beating of her heart, the motion of blood in her veins, an automatic, subconscious activity. Like a whisper. Sophie was water. And so she spoke to the ocean, and asked that it carry her.

Syrena felt the motion of a new current at the bottom of the sea. A rippling, a whirling. The girl was stretched out as if upon a magic carpet of water, thick with salt and sand, alive with primal intelligence. The water responded to Sophie as it did the moon. The girl had created a tide, and the waters rushed together and brought her forward, stopping short before the mermaid. They idled there, the harmonious interaction of a million drops of water, and Sophie could feel them all, buzzing like a hive of bees working in concert, with her as a conductor. When the current stopped short Sophie exploded into giggles.

"I *get* it!" she cheered, wild with glee. "The water is *alive!*"

"Everything is alive," Syrena nodded, pleased. "Everything is alive, and has its own magic. This you will see, my girl." The mermaid smiled so wide that Sophie caught a glimpse of the gritty baleen tucked above her teeth. "Now, you swim. Not like girl, not like mermaid. Like Odmieńce."

Chapter 7

And so the two shot off into the waters, in the direction of the North Sea, where the Swilkie spun itself atop the surface, a great white froth. Syrena pushed through the ocean with her muscular tail, her head bowed down, her arms forming a knife that cleaved the waters.

Beside her, Sophie worked the sea, not so much with her body as her mind. With great focus she commanded the waves and they carried her with a swiftness that rivaled the mermaid herself. Syrena tilted her head at her charge, smirking through the net of hair webbed in her face.

"You think you so smart now, huh? You think you faster than mermaid?" Her tail thundered behind her and she moved through the waters like pure sound.

"Ha!" Sophie spat. "You think *you're* faster than water itself?" And the current surged violently, propelling Sophie forward and knocking Syrena off course with the strength of its waves.

"Okay, okay!" the mermaid tumbled, waving her arms. She looked like Sophie once had, twisting dumbly in the waters. The girl felt a pang at the sight, to see such a noble, capable creature fumbling in her element. She stilled the current, feeling it treading beneath her, alive and waiting direction.

"I'm sorry!" Sophie hollered. Syrena had collected herself, smoothing her tangles against her temples and tucking the locks behind her ears. Her pride appeared to have a dent in it.

"Is okay," the mermaid grumbled. "I ask for it. I just happy you swimming, okay? Why do I care if you faster than me?"

It appeared to Sophie that the mermaid *did* care, but she politely pretended not to notice. "Syrena, were you really going to leave me out here? Or send me back to Chelsea on a dolphin or whatever?"

"If you not real magic girl, ya." She nodded. "If you not real magic, the plan not to work. You just get hurt, I get hurt, all the mermaids, everyone. You best be home, then. But"—her smile twinkled, the glow of her talisman flashing her canines—"I know you be magic girl. I always know. I just need to make you fight sometimes."

A feeling of longing swept over Sophie—she wanted to hug Syrena, but she knew the mermaid would never allow it. How she missed some tenderness! Her mother, Angel, the flutter of soft pigeon wings against her cheek. This work was *hard*. How she'd love something gentle to offset the struggle. But Syrena would not give that to her. It wasn't the mermaid's way. Sophie knew Syrena cared about her—she'd brought her to the middle of the Atlantic on her own back, fed her from the tangles of her hair. Syrena believed in her. But she wasn't going to give her a hug. Sophie pushed the need away and did her best to emulate the mermaid—proud, tough, cool. Syrena was cool, Sophie realized. Like, probably the coolest person Sophie'd ever met. Well, not "person," exactly, but still.

"Know what would be nice thing?" Syrena asked. "You make current a little wider, you tell water to come over to me too, ya? We both get there much faster. You do this?"

"I don't know if I can," Sophie said.

"Stop with that," the mermaid said. "You Odmieńce, you do anything. You must remember, never doubt. Doubting make you human. Knowing make you Odmieńce. Doing make you Odmieńce. Okay?"

"Yeah, sure," Sophie said, embarrassed at how quickly she turned back into a dumb, thirteen-year-old human. All it took was one challenge for her to dissolve into insecurity. Forget learning how to wall off her thoughts, or how to command the waters. What Sophie needed to learn was *confidence*.

So she did not ask, she told the waters to spread out around her, to catch Syrena in their current. And the water did her bidding.

As the two were carried toward the North Sea, Syrena slowed her motions and Sophie became entranced, watching the hypnotic roll of the creature's torso and tail as she coasted along the waters. *Cruise control*, Sophie thought, and giggled. Her mother had been so excited when she'd gotten a car with cruise control. The feature had broken on the thirdhand car not too long after she'd bought it, but Sophie still remembered her mother's delight. Something about not having to work so hard. About getting to relax while the vehicle picked up the slack. When Sophie was done with all this she'd teach her mother to talk to the air, she'd show her how to fly. Or at the very least, she'd get her a new car.

SOMETHING THE MERMAID had said was haunting Sophie, something about her time on the land. What had she said? *Was very terrible.* She wanted to ask the creature to elaborate, but felt sheepish. Even though it felt like a magical fairy tale Syrena was spinning, it wasn't. It was her *life.* Just like the talking pigeons of Chelsea weren't myths at all but part of Sophie's own half-human life. Just like the story of her grandfather, turned into a dog. Not a story at all. *Real.* Sophie realized she had much more in common with Syrena—with a mermaid—than she would ever have thought.

As if the mermaid was in her mind, reading her thoughts, Syrena turned to Sophie. "Where I leave off?" she mumbled. "Oh, yes. The mermaids leaving their eggs to the waters. The foam that came up in their mouths. It taste so bad to eat the foam!" the mermaid cried. "Some mermaids try just to spit it out, but the foam, it will find the eggs, and protect them. Is what foam meant to do. Then you have half-protected eggs, growing, only to be killed when bigger. Much sadder. Much, much sadder."

Syrena's thoughts filled with the memory of the nest of mermaid eggs that had managed to survive on the edge of the village. Patched with just

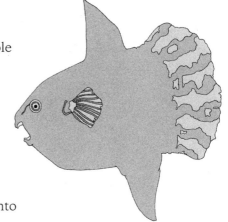

enough foam, they had gestated in a hole in the coral that had been abandoned by an eel. They grew to a hopeful size, and it was then, just as they were making their way into the village, that the sunfish attacked them. The sunfish is all head, all terrible, gobbling head, and it took the baby mermaids into its beak and tore at them. They looked like moons in the water, terrible moons sucking the baby mermaids back into their jaws and again spitting them out, doing this over and over until they were small enough for the fish to swallow.

The grown mermaids huddled and screamed. Some flung spears at the wide, round fish, but their spears sunk harmlessly into the water. The elder mermaids had stayed the hands of the ones who'd tried to kill the fish. "They weren't supposed to live," one said, sad and stern. "Don't make it harder."

Young Syrena had huddled beside her sister. Before that day, how Syrena had loved the goofy sunfish, with its one giant fin on the top of its head and another beneath. Before Syrena had ever seen the sun, this beast was its golden image. But now it was nothing more than a monster to her. Syrena cried, hiding her face in her sister's greenish-golden tangles.

"Now, now," the mermaid who cared for Syrena tried to calm her at night, wrapping her in a blanket woven from mermaid hair and seaweed, then tucking her into a clamshell. "The sunfish can't hurt you, you're much too big!"

"They're horrible!" the young mermaid wailed. "I hate them!"

"They're just living, as we all are. Think of how the fish must hate us for eating them. Think of the clams and the crabs and the lobsters."

Eventually, Syrena fell into a sleep thick with nightmares, dreaming of giant heads with tiny, vicious mouths, floating toward her. She would always hate the sunfish.

THOUGH THE ELDER mermaids thought Syrena and her sister spoiled, they couldn't stop the village from indulging them. It would be too cruel. Many of the mermaids doted upon the pair, teaching them mermaid ways—how to sing their songs and tend to their tails, where to find food and which bones and shells to collect for necessary things, like tools and weapons, but also for beauty, to decorate and ornament. They taught Syrena and her sister how and where to hide, from sharks, from ships, from humans, and, for Syrena, from the sunfish that still terrified her.

It was in Syrena and Griet's fiftieth year—when they were no longer babies but not quite full grown—that the Great War came to their waters. The mermaids who kept watch at the furthest ends of the village saw the ships approaching, and the low cries they sounded to alert the others grew as they twined together, surging into a wail that froze each mermaid in her task. This wasn't a common warning from just one corner, alerting of a passing ship. This was a siren coming from every edge of the village, raising the alarm. Could ships really be coming in from so many directions?

They were. The ships came swiftly, dropping anchor in the middle of the mermaids' village. Syrena and Griet clutched each other's hands, their eyes cast to the water's surface, where the giant curves of metal and their lengths of clattering chain crashed through. Mermaids darted away from the plummeting objects, but the anchors smashed through the intricate seashell roofs of their homes and gathering places.

Before the mermaids could begin to register the destruction, the humans in the ships began their fight. The ceiling of the mermaids' world, the watery surface that rolled with waves, refracting beams of sunlight, that hazy, shifting blue, was torn in a blast of thunder. Cannon shot pierced their sky and sunk into the village, crumbling more homes. The humans seemed committed to killing not only one another but whatever got in the way of their warring, be it mermaids or whales or gulls or dolphins. The waters became clouded with blooms of red, calling scavenging sharks to join the carnage.

Swiftly the mermaids tied protective shells around their bodies and took up rocks as shields. "To the trenches!" one mermaid hollered, and the villagers beat their tails toward the protective hollows they had dug when they first settled the bank. Debris rained all around them—chunks of wood from the prows of boats, dislodged guns, the sinking bodies of dead sailors. The mermaids swam furiously, dodging the flotsam and jetsam, dodging the cannon fire that seemed never to cease, not for a moment. From above the waves they could hear the men's gruff screams and the creaking of ships being torn apart.

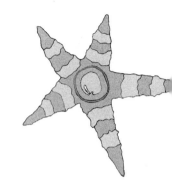

Syrena held her sister's hand and darted quickly toward the trenches, daring to look back at her village only once as she swam. Where the intricate and elegant dwellings of shells and bones and loops of rope once stood was now home to a sunken ship, alive with the struggles of drowning humans, a swirl of earthly objects spinning in the wet chaos. She faced forward to see a new ship cutting the waters right before her, and with a gasp she let go of her sister, pushing away from the ship's violent passage.

"Griet!" Syrena called to her sister, but the ship was already between them. "Griet!" she shouted, paddling her tail frantically so as to not be sucked beneath the vessel. The ships were more beastly than the most gobbling sea creature; they were not like animals that could be battled on their own terms but something else, a whole world crashing into the mermaids' world, a planet bringing its own weather down into the waters.

SYRENA DID NOT even know she was crying for her sister until she arrived at the trenches and found little Griet huddled in a corner by a pile of fishing nets, sucking on the arm of a starfish. "Griet!" she cried as she pushed toward her through the waters. She swept her sister up with her tail and buried her face in her hair, golden-green to Syrena's blue-black but equally as tangled. The starfish in Griet's grasp detached the arm the mermaid chewed upon, and she handed the rest of the creature to her sister. The two little mermaids sat in the dense mud, nervously nibbling while they clasped each other's hands feverishly.

Around them, the trench was crammed with claustrophobic mermaids hugging their tails to their chests to make room for one another. The ocean around them was alive with new currents, not born of the moon and her tugging but of the terrible boats cutting up the waters that were once the mermaids' home. Their place of safety was quickly filling up with ships en route to the fighting, their prows jammed into the thick mud, and the sailors above them howled with fury, cursing the sea devils who'd caught their mighty vessels. Some of the mermaids swam upward to try to free the boats, but their heaving was for nothing. They were great as islands, impossible to move.

"We cannot stay here!" cried an elder mermaid. "The ships are everywhere, and though they be not for us, they will show no mercy to any living creature!"

"Scatter!" hollered the toughest mermaid, the one whose tail scars were so numerous they formed a new pattern on her body. "We haven't the time for a plan! Swim for your lives, sisters, and return when the waters are clear." And as new cannon shot punctured the waters above them, the mermaids swam off in every direction, many of them into the very heart of the fighting, fewer of them into the unknown blue

of the deep, the warrior yelling after them, "Remember your home. Do not forget!"

SO, SYRENA HAD set off alone with her sister. *Griet*: the word meant pearl, and Sophie could not help but imagine Griet as opalescent, a shinier, sweeter Syrena, her curls bouncy, like a mermaid in a book.

"Was she lovely?" Sophie asked the mermaid. They had hunkered down for a rest at the northernmost edge of the Atlantic.

"We are so close to the Swilkie," Syrena mused, ignoring her question, "the whirlpool the Ogresses make with their mill. If you are very, very still you can feel the water churning." She paused. "And taste." The mermaid swished the water around inside her mouth and swallowed. "Very more salt. Good for you, ya? Ogresses have been milling salt on giant mill since they were very little girls. Wicked king take them, think they full-grown women, ya? Because they so big! He make them work and work, and then they grow up and king like, 'Uh-oh, giant ladies!' They get rid of him, but they know the sea need the salt. The whole planet do. So they keep the mill going. Very good of them, Ogresses very good people. The churning of the mill make a giant whirlpool in the sea, the Swilkie. That how we get to the Ogresses. We swim the Swilkie."

"Syrena," Sophie nagged. Even the story of the giantesses couldn't shake the tale of the mermaid's sister from her mind. "Please, tell me about Griet. Was she beautiful?"

"Oh, ya, so beautiful," Syrena answered. "The fishes swim up and kiss her pretty cheeks and seahorses comb her long hair with their tails. She wear necklace of diamond and pearl and dolphin always clean her so never the sea mud make her dirty."

Sophie listened, waiting for the mermaid to continue with the enchanting story. Instead, laughter bubbles rolled from Syrena's mouth like a school of jellyfish.

"Oh, you still such *girl*," the mermaid said. "You think everything, what you call, fairy story!"

"Well, yeah!" Sophie snapped defensively. "I mean, that's what fairy tales are. Mermaids and stuff. Pardon me for being a human."

"Griet very pretty," Syrena said, her tone slightly teasing. "All mermaid pretty. But also—she have fangs."

"Fangs?"

"Ya, like these," the mermaid opened her mouth and tapped her own long canines. "But more, longer than normal. They poke out, make her funny looking. Her hair, because so light, show more algae, look more like slime. Her tail very wonderful, sort of pink, but very hurt too, from war, and sharks."

"Sharks?"

"Ya." For the first time, the mermaid sounded tired. "When we swim away from our village, through the ships and the fighting, there be many sharks. Drawn to the fighting, all the blood. We fight them off, we dodge ships, we dodge cannons, even the dying sailors." Syrena twisted her tail, bringing Sophie's attention to a long, raised scar along its back. "This from anchor chain. The chain cracked, rough, and I become tangled. I thought I would stay forever. Griet help me. Like I help her with shark."

"What did you do?"

"Kill shark," Syrena smiled. "Kill shark and eat shark and swim good and healthy out from the sea and all the fighting."

Sophie knew that Griet didn't look like a Barbie princess mermaid doll any more than Syrena did, but she also knew that the mermaid must have been beautiful, just like the one in front of her. "And then what?" she asked. Syrena's face grew dark at Sophie's insistence, darker and suddenly older. Still beautiful, always beautiful, but it was a beauty that Sophie didn't completely understand. A beauty that scared her a little.

"Time for sleep now," Syrena said sternly. "No more 'this-is-mermaid-life.' Tomorrow we reach the Swilkie. Last time in Swilkie, almost lost fin!" The mermaid fingered the delicate scales of her hip fin gingerly. "Very athletic, Swilkie. Rest up."

"I have a sister too," Sophie surprised herself by saying. It was the first time she had spoken the truth out loud. *I have a sister.* "A twin."

Syrena spun her head to gaze at the girl, her hair following slowly, rotating like a big, black cloud above her. "Oh, no," she said. "You say there two of you?"

Sophie nodded.

"What her name?" Syrena asked. "Is she beautiful?" Sophie realized the mermaid was teasing her.

"She's—she's captured. Or something. By Kishka. She lives in Kishka's trailer at the dump."

"What 'trailer'?"

"It's like a really little space, on wheels. But it's so weird. From the outside, the space is little, but then inside it's big. Like, magic-big. And there's a garden there, but there's something wrong with it. Like the leaves are poison. When I went inside, it was like I couldn't breathe, like the plants were stealing my breath. She's trapped in there—she's been living there, inside all the plants and trees. She's so small. I think there's something really wrong with her." The memory of it made her feel sickened and sad. "It was supposed to be me in there. Kishka was tricked into taking her."

"That good story," Syrena said grimly. "That make me happy, that Kishka can be tricked." Though as she said it the mermaid sounded anything but happy. She sounded like Sophie felt: like there was a rock where her heart should be.

"I don't even know her name," Sophie said. "And I don't know if she's beautiful. She looked sick. Her skin was green, like the leaves had rubbed off on her."

Syrena swooped her long tail around Sophie and brought her close. They lay there, side by side but each far away with thoughts of their lost sisters.

Chapter 8

Eventually Syrena fell asleep, but Sophie couldn't. She tried hunkering into the mud like a cat or a mermaid, but the sand felt itchy, and she was too aware of every little fish that swam by her face. After lying there in the dark for what felt like hours, she decided to explore.

How many days had she spent at the bottom of the sea, practically traversing the whole Atlantic Ocean—and had Sophie even done any exploring? Could she even say she'd seen the deep sea? Or had she just rushed through it at the urging of a tyrannical mermaid?

Following the steady blue glow of her talisman, Sophie set out cautiously, part walking, part human-style swimming. As she paddled around, she came upon a cluster of coral dotted with slumbering sea snails. Her stomach growled at the sight of them and she nearly burst out laughing. Sea snails? Maybe she truly was becoming part mermaid. Sophie swished over to the rocks and plucked a spiral snail shell from its shallow crack. Before she could even consider the creature inside, she held the shell to her mouth, slurped, and swallowed. The snail left a slime of flavor upon her tongue, and it made her curious. She pulled another from the crack and slurped it from its home. Cruel, a voice rang in Sophie's head. It was cruel to pick the innocent snails from their resting place and end their peaceful lives so suddenly in her belly. It was cruel, like the sunfish eating the mermaids, like Syrena eating the shark. The entire ocean was cruel, and all of the earth, and Sophie was a part of it, made to consume life the way sharks were, the way the snails themselves feasted on fish killed and abandoned by other fish.

Sophie grew dizzy with the thought. She lifted the edge of her T-shirt—once boldly striped, now faded as pale as a fish bone from her time in the salty sea. She dabbed her mouth with the hem. The food chain, or rather chains, the millions of strands of life consuming life upon the planet, was suddenly something Sophie understood, more deeply than she ever had in a classroom. She held an empty periwinkle shell, covered with something fuzzy and nutritious, up to the baby

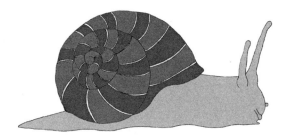

octopus still residing on her head. He grabbed it with his tentacles and went to work scraping it clean.

Sophie moved deeper into the reef, running her hands over the ruffled lids of giant clams furred with pink algae. She was mesmerized by the pulsing, colorful mantle peeking out from the shell's wide curves. Even more mesmerizing was a giant oyster nestled among them, flatter and wider than the clams, its ridged shell sprawling in all directions. Sophie had never heard of giant oysters, but what did that matter? She hadn't heard of mermaid-eating sunfish, either. As she moved closer to the oyster, its shell began to lift open in greeting. The shiny sea plants and elegant sea fans fluttered with the giant oyster's movement, and gazing at it with apprehension and wonder, Sophie could see the gleam of something dazzling on the oyster's fleshy lip. A pearl! As the oyster cranked its shell ever wider, the pearl caught the scant light available at such depths—the blue of Sophie's talisman, the luminescence of a passing worm, the sparkles of phosphorescence among the algae—and glowed, majestic and ghostly.

Griet! Sophie thought again of Syrena's sister, not that the creature had really left her mind. In fact, wasn't she somehow seeking Griet in her solo outing? With the mysterious mermaid haunting her mind, didn't she set out to find something—some proof of her left behind in this, her undersea queendom? And here it was, a giant ball of beauty in the plush body of the huge oyster. It was for this thing that Syrena's sister had been named; such a creature had to be dazzling. What must it be like to have a sister lovely as a pearl?

For lovely as a pearl Sophie's sister was not. Dumb as a plant, more like, stuck inside her grandmother's trailer, the toxic greenery binding her like roots clutching soil. Sophie shook the thought from her mind. The memory of that glimpse of her sister was truly haunting—spooky. All alone in the dark, she'd much rather imagine Syrena's sister, the beautiful Griet.

Sophie swam toward the pearl. She could gather it in her arms and carry it back to Syrena and perhaps it would comfort her. Not that the mermaid needed comfort, exactly—she seemed beyond it. But maybe in the giant pearl Syrena would see an unusual beauty, and understand for a moment the way her stories had captured Sophie's heart.

As Sophie approached its lip, it was as if the oyster inhaled, took a deep and terrible breath, pulling Sophie into its shell, sliding her across the smooth surface of the giant pearl. Sophie tried to swim against the strong current, but she was pulled completely inside the giant oyster almost immediately. And then the shell slammed shut.

Chapter 9

Sophie had never even eaten an oyster, so she didn't understand what this particular enormous one could have against her. Inside the chamber of its clamped shell, lit blue with the glow of her talisman, she tried not to panic. Which was hard, because not only was she trapped, but the oyster itself, its phlegmy body, was sticking to her in a rather disgusting way. It was like its goo was trying to cuddle with her. Wherever Sophie's body was in contact with the gooey bivalve it began sliming itself up her. It felt like living glue, impossible to peel away. She struggled against it, the groans of her effort echoing off the shell.

"Syrena!" she cried to the mermaid. Surely Syrena wouldn't be scared of a deranged oyster, even a supersized one. Syrena had battled sharks! She would rescue her. "Syrena!" she cried again—and the oyster slid a stretch of slime into her mouth, grasping and steadying her tongue.

"No use hollering," Kishka said. "You're just going to give me a headache. The acoustics in this place, oy vey."

Sophie struggled to raise her head, and she could just make out the outline of her grandmother. Kishka ashed her cigarette from atop her perch on the great pearl. Sophie grasped the terrible tentacle that was lassoing her tongue, and with all her might she tugged it free. She gagged on the taste the thing left behind, alarmed at how quickly the oyster had wrapped itself around her wrists, binding them.

"Nana!" Sophie gasped.

"Oh, don't 'Nana' me," Kishka snapped. The oyster shell was filling with the smoke from her cigarette, and Sophie choked a little on it.

"You had your chance to be a granddaughter," Kishka continued, taking a long drag off the long cigarette. In the smoky haze, Sophie squinted. The cigarette looked like it was half a foot long. Half a foot long and growing by the second. With every inhalation, the evil thing stretched further toward Sophie. Its nauseous stink and glowing orange tip slid so close Sophie could feel its heat on her face.

"Oh, you had your chance," Kishka half sang. "You could have been my little duckling, my little helper. You could have been just a sweet girl who minded her own business. Or you could have been mine. My special assistant. Sophie, the things we could have *done* together!" Kishka tapped the end of her cigarette, and a wall of ash fell inches away from Sophie's lap, sizzling in the wetness of the oyster. "Instead, I'm stuck with your sister. Dumb as a post, less of a pet than a goldfish."

It was exhausting to struggle against the sticky meat of the oyster, but every time she tried to rest, the thing increased its hold on her. She could feel it tugging at the pouch on her hip, knotted to her belt loop and full of charms from her aunt Hennie. Hennie the Winter Witch, Hennie the good. But Hennie would be no help to her here, at the bottom of the sea, a place without seasons. Sophie twisted her hips, thwarting the thing's grasp. She took a gulp of air and sputtered into a cough.

"Oh, is this bothering you, my dear?' Kishka looked at her cigarette with a bemused expression. "You know, I really *should* quit. A terrible habit. Here." The cigarette shrank back to normal size with Kishka's final drag, and Sophie watched with horror as her grandmother stubbed the burning tip out on the palm of her hand and tossed it behind her. She clapped her hands together, brushing the ash away.

"Things don't *hurt* me, Sophie. Something you should think about." Kishka looked down at Sophie, smirking. The oyster muck, whatever it was—for by now Sophie knew she'd been terribly tricked, and that of course oysters did not grow to such sizes, nor produce such majestic pearls—had attached itself to her talisman, blotting out the blue light as it slimed over the sea glass. Sophie should have known from the start that this was her grandmother. A glamour, a treacherous illusion.

"You know, I used to beat myself up, Sophie," the woman began. "For years, for years, I've been furious with myself about this. To be so powerful, and still, goodness escapes me. I just can't seem to see it. It's my giant blind spot. Now, evil, I see. Evil, I understand. Give me a war, give me a famine, give me that any day. I see it, I feed it, it feeds me. I'm happy. But goodness—it's like it doesn't exist. So I hope. I make my best guesses. Take your mother. You remember her?"

"Of course," Sophie sputtered. The oyster was climbing the cord of her talisman like a vine climbing a trellis.

"'Of course.' The woman who raised you! Well, I couldn't be sure, the way you just *abandoned* her in Chelsea, with so many terrible things happening. I thought you were maybe trying to put her out of your mind."

"Of course not! I love my mother!"

"'Love.'" Kishka chuckled. "Now, sometimes I don't see love because I'm too hateful, but sometimes, Sophia, I don't see love because it isn't there. You do not love your mother. Nor do you love your sister, that wasteling. You love nothing."

"I do!" Sophie cried, twitching her whole body in a vain attempt to shake the crawling slime from her talisman. It was wrapped around the whole cord now, and slowly climbing up her neck, as if it would lift it off her body. "No!" Sophie shouted, both at the oyster and at her grandmother, whose movements she could feel within her, deep in her heart, the place where all her feelings lived, the good and the bad. The place where her love for her mother was, and the place where her anger and disappointment lived, too. The place where a long-lost, primal love for her sister lived, a love formed in the womb but stolen soon after. She could feel Kishka's mind scraping at it, like she was trying to pick a lock. "No!" she cried, and brought the hard wall inside her up around her heart. If only she had such a mechanism to protect her body from the oyster. As her talisman floated above her face she opened her mouth and clamped her teeth around it.

"Well, if you think your mother disappointed you, imagine how I feel!" Kishka scoffed. "So much magic I have, *eons* of it, and not a bit gets passed on to her. I can't help but feel that it's her own fault. There's something wrong with a creature who can't glean even a bit of magic from one so powerful as myself." Kishka sighed. "And then you came along. You, and that other one. I couldn't tell you apart, but then all humans look the same to me. You were just little squirming things, all squirmed up together. Sucking each other's fingers, doing all those grotesque things babies do." Kishka shuddered, and Sophie felt tears spring to her eyes. She bit down harder on the oyster-covered cord of her talisman, biting against the sadness. Her sister. Once they had loved each other, in the simple way only twin baby sisters could. They had been created together, two from one. Was that sad ache she had lived with for so long, so constant she had almost ceased to feel it, the feeling of her twin torn from her heart?

"I knew I couldn't strike out three times," Kishka said. "I knew one of you had the magic. But it was so good, I could hardly see it. Then you started with the salt, tipping over the saltshaker and licking it off the table. And I knew you were the one."

Kishka slid down off the pearl, walking through the muck to where Sophie was struggling. Of course the oyster didn't cling to Kishka, not at all. Her open-toed sandals moved easily through it. She stroked her granddaughter's head gently.

"Your mother tried to trick me, you know. She tried feeding the salt to your sister, too. To confuse me. God, that woman has *no* magic," Kishka laughed a bitter laugh. "As if I couldn't see the way your sister spat it out, the way you loved it. But she tried, your mother. She almost killed your sister, feeding her salt." Kishka paused, as if deep in memory. "But that's not how I lost you. It was Hennie who did that."

"Hennie?" Sophie gurgled through her teeth, trying not to choke on the bits of oyster that fell down her open throat. What *was* this stuff? Was it going to strangle her from the inside?

"She switched you at the last minute, like a damn Boginki. I got your useless, salt-addled sister, and you—you went free."

Like a muscle flexing, Sophie felt the oyster increase its grip on her talisman, pulling it through her teeth. Like a wild dog she bit harder, shaking the cord like prey.

"When that thing comes off your head, you'll drown," Kishka said calmly. "It's the only thing letting you breathe down here. All the salt in this water isn't going to help you, my dear. Are you ready to drown?"

Sophie's eyes widened as her grip on the talisman started to fail.

"I hear it's not so bad, as far as human dying goes," Kishka said. "Peaceful. Like sleeping." She squinted at the girl. "I bet you haven't had a good night's sleep in a long time, Sophie. Wouldn't it be nice to relax? To just... float away?"

Terror surged through Sophie. She hated the whine that came through her throat as she worked to hold on to her talisman. Such a desperate sound, a whinny. The sound of an animal losing a fight.

"Of course, you could always make my dream come true. Be the granddaughter I've always wanted. It's much, much easier to make a good person bad than to make a bad person good. You'll never get anywhere with me, dearie. But what I could do with you! You could be awful. We could make war together. We could destroy the whole world."

The talisman rose higher, the sea glass now in the air above Sophie's head, floating like a balloon. Sophie arched her neck, clenching the cord in her teeth.

"Just let down that wall around your heart and show me, Sophie. Show your grandmother you mean it. That you'll work with me, that you'll be my special dearie."

None of this is real, none of this is real, Sophie said to herself, her mind frantic inside her head. So if it wasn't a real shell, a real pearl, if the thing sucking at her wasn't a real oyster, what was it? A manifestation of Kishka's mind? She remembered how Hennie had set up the feast to welcome her, the perfumed elixirs and chocolate-chip cookies. And Sophie had blown Hennie away, hadn't she? For once the memory didn't shame her, how in her frustration and confusion, overwhelmed by all she was learning about her history, about her family, she had lashed out against her kindly aunt, destroying her home. This time the memory inspired her. If she could out-magic Hennie, she had to at least try it on her grandmother. She knew Kishka was more powerful than Hennie, her sister. But Sophie didn't want to drown, and she didn't want to go with her grandmother, to fall down that tunnel

of horror and pain, and to *like* it. The thought made Sophie's goodness, her magic, rear up inside of her like a horse. And inside of this
magic, Sophie realized, was everything she needed.

First, Sophie would become a shark. Why not? The understanding
that she could do this, become something else, a creature as powerful
as a *shark*, filled her with such delirious delight that she laughed out
loud. And when she laughed, her mouth opened wide, and when her
mouth opened wide the talisman began to float away from her, the cord
hovering for a moment in the dark space of her mouth.

Then the shark teeth came.

Row upon row of them sliced up through Sophie's gums, piercing
the cord between their vicious peaks like a bit of dental floss.

The flicker of shock Kishka felt as her granddaughter morphed into
a great white was all it took for her glamour to fizzle, like the plug had
been pulled on a giant neon sign. In an instant the oyster was gone,
and so was the pearl; the shell was gone, and all the groping, gooey
muck. And then Sophie's grandmother was gone. Where she had been
sitting, there was not an old woman in a flowered housecoat, but a sea-
beast like nothing Sophie had ever seen. It looked like a great, scaled
snake with a face sprouting poisoned tentacles long and droopy as a
catfish's whiskers. Its eyes were as big as giant clams, and Sophie knew
not to look into them. In their depths swirled all the pain of the world,
electric and alive. Sophie swam up above the monster and with an
instinct she hadn't known before she sunk her razored jaw deep into
the neck of the Odmieńce.

God, her grandmother tasted terrible! The juices of this beast—blood or bile or evil itself, whatever it was, it stung and sickened Sophie, and try as she might she had to pull back. She clamped shut her great jaw as she did, tearing a chunk of the beast and spitting it into the waters. As the monster twisted away from her, strands of its torn flesh spinning around its body, Sophie went in again, this new instinct powerful inside her. As fast as a bullet she dove, and with a chomp of her massive jaw she severed the head of the beast from its undulating tail.

More sharks had come, real ones, Sophie could tell, not teenage girls pretending to be sharks. But was it pretend? Sophie could feel her body, thick as a tank but weightless in the water. And the instinct for blood was inside her, a reflex, always ready. Sophie watched the feeding frenzy as the sharks lit upon the sinking tail. And the head, the terrible, disembodied head turned to face Sophie, and for a moment it was not the head of a sea-dragon but the decapitated head of an old woman, her grandmother.

"Now you've done it," Kishka spoke, with a grimace that tore at Sophie's still-human heart.

"Oh!" she cried, and tried to swim toward her grandmother. But the head again became a dragon's, and its tentacle caressed her face, and Sophie screamed a zawolanie thick with surprise and pain and anger. Sophie's zawolanie burst through her jaw, exiting her mouth in an explosion of shark teeth. It rippled outward all around her in a blast, and somewhere on the northernmost edge of the Atlantic Ocean a rogue wave rose and smashed back into the waters.

Chapter 10

A roar of sound woke Syrena, and she opened her eyes to a current so strong she could *see* it, the movement of the water rushing toward her, scooping her up and carrying her away in its rocketing velocity. For a mile or so the mermaid fought the water, tumbling and scratching in a manner alien to her species. Syrena had lived in the ocean for hundreds of years, and rarely had she felt out of sorts within its waters. It was more like her skin than her home, and she knew all its secrets. It felt like a rogue wave was building on the surface above.

At last Syrena was able to swim out from the current, and she turned back toward her charge, her great tail slamming the waters. Schools of fish divided themselves at the sight of her, giving her space to speed through. She finally came upon the girl hunched over by a bed of giant clams, retching. A pile of half-digested periwinkles sat in the mud by her feet, picked at by small, scavenging fish.

"Gross," Sophie mumbled, turning away from her mess. When she saw Syrena, she waved her hands wildly through the water. "Did you see all that?"

Syrena shook her head. "No, but a terrible current woke me."

"You *slept* through that? You slept through me becoming a *shark* and biting my grandmother's head off?" Sophie cracked up, disturbing the mermaid with her cackle. She sounded mad. Syrena surveyed the reef.

"I see nothing," she said. "Just strange girl and upchucked sea snail. You eat bad mollusk, have bad dreams?"

"Oh yeah, it was a bad dream all right." Sophie kicked sand onto the periwinkle pile, scattering the tiny fishes. "The worst. I wound up trapped inside a giant fake oyster with my grandmother, who was *smoking* this endless *cigarette*, and the oyster was, like, this *thing* that was trying to steal my talisman so I'd *drown*, and so I became a shark and bit her head off, and then got freaked out and then she was this, like, sea monster and her whisker hit me, and look—" Sophie turned her cheek to the mermaid. She didn't know what it looked like, but the throb of it was hot and constant upon her face. Syrena peered at the wound.

"Look like jellyfish sting," she said. "I see worse."

"Yeah, well, it was the whiskers of this water dragon or whatever my grandmother was. And it hurt so bad I let out a zawolanie I wasn't even expecting, and all my shark teeth blew out of my mouth and now my jaw totally hurts. Do I have all my teeth?" She opened her mouth wide for the mermaid.

"Not get too close," the mermaid put her hands up to stop Sophie's advance. "Smell pukey, can smell from here. You dream you puke shark teeth, wake up to upchuck?"

"God, Syrena, it was Kishka! You know how crazy and powerful she is. You know she's out to get me. She was trying to kill me."

"I know, I know. Shhhhhhhhh." Syrena made a low hissing noise and reached out and petted Sophie's head. Sophie was immediately comforted, lulled by the noise and the gentle, electric touch of the mermaid's fingers on her scalp. The tension that had clenched her body into one too-tight, girl-sized muscle began to relax, but her body was still vibrating with the shock of her zawolanie, her face still stung from her beastly grandmother, and her jaw ached with the effort of shifting from girl teeth to shark teeth to exploded teeth, and then back to girl.

Sophie closed her eyes. "You're putting me to sleep," she murmured, drifting in the water like a sea fan.

"You in bit of shock. Too much for you, all of it. My sound good, relaxing sound. Good tones."

"Mermaid magic," Sophie said.

Syrena laughed. "Magic just science. Just science not discovered by men in silly jackets yet."

"No," Sophie insisted gently. "Mermaids are magic."

"Humans think so, but stupid. You find new lemur in jungle, you think magic lemur? No. Just a hiding lemur. Mermaids hiding creatures. Natural, like you or lemur, or dolphin. We just secret animal."

"But you talk about magic, mermaid magic—"

"Ya, but not like you think. All creatures have their magic. Again, is science."

"So, magic isn't magic, it's science?" A conversation that at any other time would have frustrated and confused Sophie was turned into a sweet riddle by the humming of the mermaid and the feel of her head massage.

"Ya, just another thing, like sound, like gravity."

"Okay," Sophie said.

"Don't be so—how to say—bummed out. Magic still what it is, no matter what."

"I feel like you're sort of taking the fun out of it," Sophie said.

"Shhhhhhhhhhhhhh," Syrena sounded another tone.

It's her zawolanie, Sophie thought. *Mermaid magic is all zawolanie, they're zawolanie creatures, hurting and healing with sound.*

"I think you maybe traumatized." Syrena curled her tail around the girl in a rare gesture of sympathy. "And your pretty face hurt now."

"I think I almost died!" A surge of feeling came up inside her, and Sophie burst into unexpected tears. "She almost took this." She clutched her talisman, the blue glowing out from between her fingers. "I would have drowned."

The mermaid considered the talisman, petting her own. "I can breathe fine without talisman."

"Well, you're a mermaid."

"Ya, but you part Odmieńce. You become shark, you can figure to breathe underwater."

"How?"

"Don't ask me," Syrena shrugged. "But you command the waters, ya? You have them carry you? They do what you ask. Ask them for oxygen."

"Oh, hey, water, can you give me some oxygen?" Sophie called out into the deep. She paused, yawned. "Hmmm, don't really see any oxygen coming my way."

"I believe you do it," Syrena said simply. "You be brat, fine. But I believe you take oxygen from the water. Is your magic, your science, what you wish to call it."

And with that, Syrena removed the comfort of her tail from the girl and beat it gently in the waters. "Come now. We must visit Swilkie. We not on—what you call—vacation down here."

"Yeah, trust me, I know," Sophie said, already missing Syrena's soothing touch. "Almost getting murdered by my grandmother in a disgusting oyster shell is not exactly a trip to Disney."

"What is 'Disney'?" Syrena asked.

"Oh, god, it's—it's too much to explain. It's like a big fun park kids go on vacation to. Plus they make movies and stuff. Actually, they have a movie about a mermaid—" Sophie stopped talking as some of Syrena's words about Griet floated through her head. "Oh geez," she said out loud in a sickened voice.

"Oh, what, they make bad mermaid movie, ya?" Syrena saw the answer in Sophie's downturned face. "Let me guess," she said in a hard voice. "They make movie about my sister?"

Sophie nodded. Syrena sighed, releasing a column of shimmering air bubbles, but Sophie could see her face behind it, the sadness visible in her eyes, the lines around her mouth. "Griet even more famous mermaid than me. Griet most famous. The small mermaid, they call her. But Griet not even very little! Griet normal mermaid size. Oh well. That is life. Stories get confused, sometimes on purpose, sometimes by mistake. I know truth of Griet. And I tell the truth to you. So as long as you and me alive, Griet's truth alive, ya?"

"I guess so," Sophie said, but at that moment, at the bottom of the sea, still shell-shocked from the run-in with her grandmother, it didn't seem like enough. To be charged with keeping someone's story seemed like a big responsibility. And if Sophie couldn't even handle one person's story, how was she going to handle saving the world?

"Come on," Syrena said, jolting Sophie from her worries. "I see my calming spell already going away, your face look like this"—the mermaid arranged her face in a parody of Sophie's, all bulging eyes and chewed lip. "This whole trip taking too long. You must understand, longer I am away from river, longer the Boginki have chance to destroy it. More mess for me to clean when I return. Not to mention, longer we down here, less time you have in castle, to train."

"Can't you train me down here?" Sophie asked. "While we're swimming?"

The mermaid looked deeply at her charge. "I am training you. I train you in ways you don't even know. I train your heart. Now, command the waters, and I will continue my story."

*　*　*

SYRENA AND GRIET held their hands so tightly they thought perhaps they would meld together into an entirely new sea creature. Swimming in unison, each beat of their tails in perfect sync, Griet thought how wonderful it would be if she and her sister *did* become one, how much stronger they would be in this treacherous sea! Too grown to be eaten by sunfish, they were still at the mercy of sharks and some of the bigger seals. Griet imagined herself and Syrena as a two-headed sea beast, double the tail to smack and swim with and sporting starfish append-ages that dropped away when trapped. She shared her dreams with her sister, who laughed, but there was a tinge of sadness to her hap-piness. They were cut off from their village, alone, and still so young. Their gratitude for each other was tangled up with loneliness for the other mermaids.

"You have to stop dreaming," Syrena chastised Griet. "We need to find you a weapon, too."

Syrena had spotted the narwhal horn lodged in the seafloor, its tip driven deep into the sand, the hilt of it unmistakable. Her heart had leapt in her chest. Narwhal horns were rare, and only the bravest of the warrior mermaids carried one. They came to the most powerful mermaids, the ones destined to be leaders of their kind. The narwhal had not swum in the mermaids' waters for centuries, and so to find a horn was unlikely, a sign that the mermaid was meant for great things.

"Do you know what this means?" Syrena asked her sister breath-lessly. Together they studied the hollow, spiraling tusk. It was too long, unwieldy and awkward, but Syrena would master it, she was sure she

would. The narwhal tusk was *hers*, just as surely as if someone had given it to her or left it there, at the tip of Skagerrak Strait, for her and only her to find. The horn was sharp as a sword and almost as long as her tail. Syrena experimented with different ways of clutching it. She swirled around the waters, jabbing and slashing at an imaginary foe. Using her own and Griet's hair, Syrena wove a long sheath to carry the weapon and slung it across her back. Before the day's end she had used it to spear a shark that had menaced the mermaids, bringing it down in a bloody heap on the seafloor, its monstrous mouth agape.

Syrena rubbed the edge of a shell on a rock until it was so sharp the edge was nearly translucent. "Do you see?" Syrena showed Griet, who touched the knife gently and still brought away a finger beaded with blood. Syrena butchered the shark, bringing thick cuts of meat back, and the girls had a feast. Afterward Syrena cut a fearsome tooth from the shark's mouth and wound it into her hair. It flashed there in the ocean's dark light, both an ornament and a warning.

"I can't do what you do," Griet said, still shaken by what she'd seen. How evil the shark had looked, with its small, focused eyes and a mouth so wide the mermaid could have swum right into it. She shuddered. If it hadn't been for Syrena and her narwhal tusk, Griet knew she'd be lying in the beast's belly right now. Instead, it was lying in hers. The whole experience had left her queasy.

When she lived in the village, Griet hadn't needed to be everything. No single mermaid had: each could do what came to her naturally, braiding or singing or helping build houses. Griet didn't like to fight or hunt, and though she was elegant with the instruments the mermaids built from fish bones and seashells and seal leather and coral, she was not elegant with a weapon. She was clumsy. In the village, it hadn't mattered. Whatever she couldn't do, another mermaid could, and they all worked together to have what they required. But here, alone with her sister, the ocean required her to be everything—hunter and butcher and explorer and builder. She looked at her sister with hurt and amazement. "Even if I had a narwhal horn I couldn't do what you do, Syrena."

"Well, you can do something," Syrena insisted. "And you've got to have something to defend yourself with. Here." Syrena handed her sister the knife she'd just fashioned.

Griet handled it gingerly, as if it were not an object but a living thing, an unpredictable eel likely to strike out at her. "I'll probably only hurt myself with it," she mumbled, shakily bringing the blade to her long tangles and cutting into one. With nimble fingers she pulled apart the knot, then went to work weaving the strands into a holster to carry it. The knife was so sharp she had to weave it thicker and thicker, as it kept cutting through her knitwork. Griet tied the knife to her waist and looked sheepishly at her sister.

"Great!" Syrena said proudly, and Griet allowed herself a smile. Scavengers had come and surrounded the dead shark in a flickering cloud. It was time for them to move on.

"That was relaxing," Syrena said, sliding her horn back into its sheath.

"Relaxing!" Griet burst into laughter at her sister. "Only you would find it relaxing to slay a shark!"

Syrena shrugged. "We're mermaids. We do what needs to be done."

The pair continued their swim, not quite sure what they were looking for. Were they meant to find a hiding place and remain there, alone? Would the elders come for them when the war was over? How would they know when it was safe to return home? They coasted through the strait, dining on cod so plentiful all they needed was to stretch out their hands and grab them.

Eventually the Skagerrak released the mermaids into Kattegat Bay, and slowly the channel began to narrow. With the land closing in, the mermaids became nervous. Were they swimming down a dead end? With land came humans, and mermaids did not like to be so close to their settlements. But the pair had already swum so long and so hard. The thought of turning back was exhausting. And so the sisters pressed forward. Soon the roof of their world, the water's surface, grew very close. Though perhaps it was deep to humans, the bay was shallow to mermaids, and the sisters lay on their backs, floating, gazing upward. The sun warmed the water of the bay and they felt the chill leaving their skin.

"Perhaps we should peek?" Griet suggested. "Gather where it is we are?"

Syrena nodded. Her narwhal tusk was still lashed to her back, and she placed a hand on it absently, a new habit. With her other hand she reached out for Griet, and with the slightest fluttering of their tails, the mermaids rose until their heads broke the surface.

They were shocked to see how close the land was, and that among the scattered rocks and lush greenery there were tiny, colorful houses.

Human houses. Fishing boats bobbed in the distance, their sails puckering in the light wind. Enchantment lit up Griet's face. She'd never seen a human settlement, and she certainly hadn't expected it to be so like a mermaid village. The scale of the houses, the way they sat alongside each other—it swelled her heart with longing for her own home. Without thinking, she began to swim toward the rocky shore.

"Griet!" Syrena gasped. "Don't!"

"Just a little closer. Look at the colors!" A mermaid village was beautiful in its own way, fashioned of the pale shells and bones of sea creatures, furred here and there with a neon burst of algae, but mostly it was a pale and fragile construction. These little houses were boldly colored, red as shark blood and yellow as the sun, blue as the sea! Colors that looked so different outside the waters that it was as if Griet had never seen them before.

Syrena followed her sister with darkness in her heart. It was true that the settlement was charming, but Syrena could not help but be wary of the humans that dwelled there. Humans had rarely shown mermaids kindness. Their once-friendly exchanges had happened so long ago they seemed to Syrena nothing more than fairy stories. It was because of the humans that the sisters were here, lost and alone, bobbing in a bay far from their home sea. Syrena unsheathed her tusk and kept it at the ready as she paddled through the shallow waters, joining Griet at the banks.

Griet clutched at the rocks with her hands, her pearly fingertips shining in the light. Her smile was so wide Syrena couldn't even see her fangs; they blended in with the rest of her teeth. The tip of her baleen poked out from under her lip.

"Oh, don't you wish you could go there!" It wasn't a question, it was pure desire. Griet didn't even turn to her sister to see what Syrena thought; she tilted her head back to the mild sun, enjoying its rays on her bluish-white skin. Her nose flared as she inhaled the special smell of the place—the salt in the water as it dried upon the rocks, the sea plants lying stiff on the shore, kicked up by the tides. Griet reached as far as she could and plucked one from the land, brought it to her mouth with a crunch.

"Awwwwwwhhf!" She mumbled a loud, happy sound, her mouth full of seaweed. "Taste this!" she thrust it to her sister. "Have you ever tasted something like this before?"

Reluctantly, Syrena took the food. No, she hadn't ever tasted anything like it before. The heat of the sun and the dryness of the air had transformed the plant to something altogether different than it was underwater. The salt of the bay had crystallized upon it, and it crunched pleasingly between her teeth.

"When we get back to the village, I'm going to make this!" Griet cried, inspired. "We can find a rock and leave the plant in the sun! The others will love it!"

The mention of the village and the thought of feeding the others made both mermaids quiet with sadness. But as Syrena's thoughts drifted homeward, Griet tipped her head back and continued sniffing the air as if sampling food from a banquet.

"I can smell the pines over there," she said, pointing toward the cluster of deep green trees far back on the shore. "And the wood the people used for their homes. And the wood they burn, that dark smoke leaving their homes." She closed her eyes and kept breathing. And that was why she didn't see the man approaching the shore, why she was so startled to find her sister with her narwhal horn drawn as if to strike.

Chapter 11

The waters of the North Sea were cold and thick with salt. They seemed to take more effort to move through, like switching gears on a bicycle. Sophie could feel her body adjusting to the new conditions as she pushed through, water streaming around her. At first she had been cold, but like a walrus, like something that belonged down there, her body had started to adjust, and she was fine. The goose bumps that covered her arms and legs were probably permanent, but Sophie had ceased to notice them. What she did notice was the new creatures popping up in the dusky waters—the glittering spirals that shimmered up from a clump of dowdy algae, looking like the fizzing sparklers Sophie and Ella had lit on the Fourth of July.

"*Clavelina lepadiformis*," Syrena offered, noticing the girl noticing the creature. "Sea squirts. Very tasty. Tingle on the tongue."

A jellyfish red as a clown's nose pulsed by, trailing long, crimson tendrils, looking like a tropical flower. When a school of cod passed by, Syrena reached out and snagged one, her long nails puncturing its scales.

"When I girl, schools of cod so great, mermaid get lost in them! Once me and Griet separated by cod and took minutes to find one another. So many fish! Not now. Too many humans, and ocean so dirty." She took a vicious bite from the side of the fish, spitting out bones. "Not as good," she shook her head. "Don't taste like what cod used to taste."

Syrena could be so jaded, Sophie thought. The North Sea, to Sophie, was perfect and full of magic. Up ahead she spied a gang of spotted seals playing together, swimming and swirling, diving and tumbling, their whiskery noses making them look like undersea puppies.

Syrena noted the wonder on Sophie's face, and in her mermaid

way, she went about killing it. "Ya, they cute," she said coldly, "Unless you so little they try to eat you."

"Syrena!" Sophie whined. "I like them."

"I like them, too. Wrapped in seaweed, cooking by a vent in the seafloor. Delicious."

They passed over a forest of sea pens, their feathery polyps outstretched and glowing, like a stage full of burlesque dancers bearing fans and sequins. Lobsters scampered below, gazing up at the pair with eyes as blue as the sea that was their home.

"Wish I hadn't filled up on that cod," Syrena said regretfully. "I'll be back for you." The lobster rushed to hide among the coral. A minke whale, its skin elegantly ridged, its mouth impossibly long, coasted by, creating a wake that Sophie and Syrena bounced upon.

Something nagged at Sophie as she slunk through these rich, new waters. Her body still felt worn from her latest magic—her teeth loose in her mouth, her throat scorched from the fire of her zawolanie. Her stomach felt unsettled; she hadn't been able to ingest anything but a few bites of seaweed and some algae sucked from her hair. But all in all, she was okay. She had tangled with Kishka, and it seemed that she had won.

"Syrena?" Sophie called to the mermaid. "You know everything that just happened to me? With Kishka?"

"How you turn to shark and bite head off? Ya. You tell me. I wish I had seen. To see you bite Kishka! I would have cheered!"

"Well, I feel pretty good, you know? I don't feel that sick. I mean, I need to take a nap—"

"After the Swilkie, the Ogress will give you nap."

"Yeah, but I mean, my point is, how come I'm okay? Why aren't I more hurt? It was *Kishka*."

"You in ocean," the mermaid said. "You soaking in salt. You are salt, almost. You strongest here. You bathe in it, swallow it. You constantly getting salt. It heal you before you even hurt."

"Hmph." It was true that Sophie could barely taste the salt anymore. The salt had become everything, her whole world.

"You no try to look into Kishka, right?" Syrena asked. "Peek into her heart, or whatever she has? No heart, I don't think."

"No," Sophie said with a shudder. "I never, ever want to see that. Not after what you showed me." Sophie recalled the night at the creek, back in Chelsea, a million years ago it seemed. How the mermaid had given her a glimpse of all the world's pain, the deep, dark core of her grandmother. How it had knocked her straight out, scrambled her part-human, part-mortal body. She had come to puking fish and creek water and scared Ella right out of their best-friendship.

"I show you that because you need to know it," Syrena said, "And to see it direct from Kishka herself, it kill you."

"*Kill* me?" Sophie marveled.

"Yeah, kill you dead. You with no training, no salt, no nothing, just a girl, don't even know pigeons talk yet? You see Kishka's insides, you just—poof. Dead."

"What about now?" Sophie asked. "Now that I'm in the ocean all this time? Now that I can control the water?"

"Well, ya," Syrena nodded. "Probably not kill you. Probably just make you like seaweed for rest of your life. You know, you just lie there forever, nothing."

"Ugh, that's even worse!"

"Ya, ya. No worry, Sophie. We are going to make you strong as narwhal horn! Look."

In the distance before them was a white column. It even resembled the horn the mermaid had talked about, a giant, ivory spiral. But as they crept closer, Sophie slowing the waters, she saw it was more like a tornado. An underwater tornado, spinning, frothing, sucking water from the surface in a controlled frenzy.

"The Swilkie," Sophie said.

"Ya, ya, the Swilkie," Syrena nodded. "So powerful. We will swim inside."

Sophie opened her mouth to speak. *"Swim inside?"* she was going to say. "What are you talking about, *swim inside!*" The twisting tower looked violent as a swarm of sharks. But she bit her tongue. She had fought Kishka and won. Every day the ocean made her stronger, without her even knowing about it. The very waters responded to her, doing her bidding as if she were their queen. And maybe she was! Maybe she was Sophie Swankowski, Queen of the Waters. Then it was time for her to act like it. She was about to meet the Ogresses, the giant women who had dug for her the best chunk of salt the sea had to offer, a giant cube of salt that had melted down to a beautiful pearl and had saved Sophie when she was so sick. She would not act like a child. Not to them, and not to Syrena.

"How do we do it?" she asked the mermaid. Her voice was steady, and her eyes were stuck on the Swilkie. How majestic it was. Sophie wished she could linger by the storm of it and watch it twirl. Like a terrible ballet, elegant but brutal, too. Sophie did not understand how she could swim into such a thing without being torn apart. But she didn't understand how she had made herself into a shark, either. Not understanding didn't mean anything anymore. It only mattered that she was ready to learn.

"I think you make easy for us," Syrena said, "if you tell water to help. Normal, we just swim into it. And it bang us around like this and that, oh! You think periwinkles hurt your stomach! You stay caught in Swilkie for a couple days, your whole body feel like one bad stomach!"

"A couple *days*?" Sophie asked in exactly the frightened, whiny tone she was trying to avoid. She cleared her throat, hoping she could clear away some panic in the process. "I mean—so, we'll spin in the Swilkie for how long? How many days?"

"Long as take to reach center. Center of Swilkie calm, like long, calm tunnel. We swim right down to Ogresses. Very easy. But not easy to swim into center, because water push and pull you very hard, like trying to eat you."

"Huh." Sophie looked at the spinning Swilkie. Twisting, twisting, twisting, they both could feel its power, its pull. Sophie knew that all they had to do was swim a little bit closer and then the Swilkie would do the work, sucking them right in.

"But I think you maybe just ask the water to open for us," Syrena suggested. "Like, make path right to center? You try, ya?"

"How?" Sophie asked, and the mermaid gave her a look. "Okay, give me a second." Sophie focused on the water. It felt, in some strange way, like doing a math puzzle. There were patterns at work and Sophie could manipulate them. Part of it was that the water was alive, and her asking did the work. But the water was also information, streams and streams of it, and Sophie could change what it was saying, rewrite it. Her tinkering was also her asking.

If Sophie paused to think about it too clearly, she knew it wouldn't work. With her mind and with something else, her intuition perhaps, Sophie dug into the structure of the water and she divided it with a plea. In just a breath she felt what she had done. Her talisman allowed her to breathe beneath the water, but it wasn't the same. Sophie had created a pocket of oxygen. The sudden breath of it shot straight to her head, making her giddy.

"Syrena, look!" she cried. Before them was a tunnel, a strange space that cut through the water—but Sophie could see, too, that it seemed to be killing everything in its path. Sophie smacked her hand to her mouth as she watched a small school of silvery fish twitch and then, en masse, flutter to the ground like torn paper. On either side of the oxygen tunnel, swaying strips of sea grass grew brittle and brown, then crumbled. But still, they needed to make it through the Swilkie.

"Sophie, what are you doing?" Syrena cried.

Whatever it was, Sophie did it harder. She pried and unlocked the water all the way up to the Swilkie's wild column, and a gap appeared in its side.

"It's oxygen!" Sophie cried.

"You're killing the creatures!" the mermaid hollered back, as a pair of cod swam haplessly into the airy space and began to gasp, seizing and falling. Some that had lagged behind seemed to explode in a burst of silvery rain.

"Quickly, quickly, go, so I can stop it!" She pushed the mermaid in the direction of the space in the Swilkie, and the mermaid, entering the oxygen chamber, fumbled.

"I can't swim!" she cried. "There is nothing to swim in!" Like the sea creatures before her, she fumbled and flailed. She took deep breaths of oxygen and stumbled forward, Sophie pushing from behind, keeping the gate open. They were swimming clumsily upon air, Sophie holding the whole unnatural situation together with her mind, and it was exhausting. *Go, go go go go*, she thought, pushing herself forward, willing the mermaid through the portal in the Swilkie's rushing waters. All around them, the living ocean died as it encountered a combustible cloud of oxygen where seawater once flowed.

Syrena pushed into the hole in the Swilkie, and Sophie reached out and grabbed her tail, pulling herself in. The sound of the water roaring around them was deafening, like being trapped in a waterfall. As Syrena curved her body into the eye of the Swilkie, Sophie relaxed her grip on the water—and felt the Swilkie's churning wall crash down on her.

Sophie saw Syrena's face as the mermaid turned inside the serenity of the eye; watched her expression morph from relief to horror. Sophie had let go of the water too soon. She had seen the mermaid enter the eye and thought they had both arrived. She was wrong.

It was as if the sea had taken its muscular arm and wrangled the girl into a headlock, then proceeded to whip her around in a circle at a velocity she could barely comprehend. Probably she was tumbling, but it happened so fast she could not even register it. Her body felt beyond her, held in the many fists of the Swilkie. She spun and spun until her brain felt scrambled, until space and time were pounded away.

But eventually Sophie began to relax. She hadn't even known she was struggling; the wild motion of the Swilkie caught everything in its grip, making it one, and it was impossible to tell where her body ended and the waters began. But now, with her breath growing calm, Sophie began to enjoy the spinning. Its motions even seemed to slow, though Sophie knew this was impossible. She thought about how the rotations of the earth were undetectable. Had the Swilkie become her home? Would she eventually grow to not feel the whirlpool at all? Would she be stuck here forever?

The swirling water made intricate patterns around her face. Whether her eyes were open or closed, she felt their ever-shifting lace imprinted on her vision. Even the constant rush of the waters became inaudible after a time, and she spun in a dreamy quiet, acclimated to the roar completely. *Or,* a part of Sophie's mind piped up, *maybe it's made you deaf.*

It became so that Sophie could not tell when her eyes were open and when they were shut. After a few hours of this—*or maybe a year,* Sophie couldn't help but think—a movement somewhere beyond the Swilkie's froth roused her from the water's trance. It was as if something was beating against the sea in short, sharp raps. Smacking at it. A tail. Had the Swilkie sucked in a whale? Would Sophie soon be doing this endless waltz with a whale, twirling and suspended, timeless, motionless?

"Sophieeeeeeeeeeeee!" It was like hearing her name through panes of glass, through ears stuffed with cotton.

"Sophieeeeeeeeeeeee!" It was like her name was being howled by a ghost.

On the other side of the wall of water, the girl saw another flick of a tail. She saw the scratch of claws, claws that glowed like pearls. Pearls. Griet. Syrena. Syrena, her mermaid! And it was as if Sophie was waking up from something, a slumber or a fever, something that had addled her, made her dull, nearly made her forget who she was and where she was going.

"Syrena!" she screamed, and the water filled her mouth like a punch. She coughed and spit it out and it splashed back against her face, confusing her. But she couldn't afford to be confused. She tried to relax, letting the Swilkie spin her. She looked and listened, and again saw the dark motion of a tail beyond the water.

"Swim to me, Sophieeeeeeeeeeee!" The mermaid called as if from another dimension. And Sophie let her strength gather, and then called it throughout her body. With a controlled zawolanie, she rocketed herself through the wall of water, which battered at her viciously as she broke through its prison. She landed in Syrena's arms.

"Oh, I think the Swilkie keep you forever!" the mermaid cried, petting the girl's wild hair. Her hand struck a bump upon Sophie's scalp, and she pushed away a tangle to reveal the baby octopus. "You still here?" she asked the creature. Its tentacles were twined into the roots of Sophie's hair, and it too seemed rattled from the Swilkie. Sophie's shirt was torn from the power of the water, and her already ragged cutoffs were shredded.

Sophie looked up at the mermaid's face, her grayish-blue skin and wide, blue eyes that glowed like talismans. Sophie had never been to an art museum, but it seemed like the mermaid would be something you'd find in such a place. Chiseled and majestic, both beautiful and tragic. Sophie would have liked to stare at the mermaid forever, but she cast her eyes downward. Syrena didn't like being stared at, and Sophie was enjoying the mermaid's embrace too much to risk being spat out of her arms.

"How long was I in there?" she murmured into Syrena.

"Oh. A week, I think. Too long. Was so worried about you was not even bored!" the mermaid laughed her harsh laugh. "You imagine, stuck in this place? Look around you."

Sophie brought her head up and surveyed the space as she was told. It was nothing, a void. Around them the waters rushed, eternal, heedless of the creatures caught inside.

"All week I do nothing but stare at water, look for you. Stare so long, I start to see things. Stare so long, my eyes so tired, still, I stare even more, to find you."

Sophie squeezed the mermaid. She couldn't imagine what would have happened without her. She'd be there forever, spinning and spinning. Forgetting she even existed, entranced by the water. "It messed my brain up," Sophie tried to explain. "Being in there. I almost forgot you were here!"

"I very sure," the mermaid said. "Why don't you ride on my back? I take us to the Ogresses."

Gratefully, Sophie slung her arms around Syrena's neck, burying her face in the mermaid's pile of hair. Upon her own head, the baby octopus began to lessen its grip, pulling itself free of her tangles. It felt like a head massage, and Sophie almost cried, she was so happy. To go from the center of a storm to lying upon a mermaid like a hammock while a baby octopus gave you a head rub—Sophie felt in that moment that if her life was not charmed then there was no such thing as charm.

As the mermaid began to swim them through the eye of the Swilkie, Sophie struggled to keep her eyes open. A week ago she had had no idea what a Swilkie even was, and here she was in the heart of it. She should pay more attention. She would likely never be in such a place again. But with the rushing of the waters all around her, the girl was lulled to sleep.

Chapter 12

Sophie woke with a start, and then a scream. An eyeball as big as her face was peering at her, wide and golden and unblinking. The scream that left her mouth was hoarse but piercing, and Syrena was swiftly at her side, delivering a smack to her shoulder.

"Respect!" she barked. "And some gratitude, if you please!"

So much for the cozy, cuddling mermaid who'd saved her life and cradled her through the eye of the storm. Syrena was back to her old self, the cranky mermaid of the city of Warsaw who had for so long protected the city's river with little more than her bad attitude.

"I'm sorry," Sophie mumbled, rubbing her shoulder and looking down at her bedding. She was not quite awake enough to peer into the giant eye of an Ogress again. "I just—I was having a nightmare."

"It seems as if time has been one long nightmare lately, hasn't it?" asked the Ogress in a voice both booming and smooth. Sophie could tell that the creature was attempting to whisper, for her sake. Sophie took a deep breath and looked into her eye.

Well, it was a very pretty eye. Brown and gold flickering together like a light show. The Ogress pulled back a bit and Sophie could see her other eye, both of them set into a massive face. The nose was bold and the lips full and curved. Her long hair fell in a plait down her back, and Sophie was suddenly aware of her own wild snarls. She touched her hair anxiously, and her hand bumped something scratchy. Livia's feather. Her hair had wound around it so densely Sophie would have to cut it out if she ever wanted to remove it—which she never, ever would.

She fingered it, feeling the love she felt for the bird in her heart. If Livia were alive, were with her, she would urge Sophie to be brave, brave and well-mannered. The feather dangling in her hair would remind her of that always, would help her live up to the person her pigeon friend had believed her to be.

And what of all the others she'd left behind? What would Ella say if she saw her now, sleeping in a place so far beneath the sea she bet no other human had visited? *But I'm not human*, she answered herself. She couldn't wait to tell her best friend the news: *Hey, guess what, I'm not even totally human!* She could imagine Ella making a joke and giving her a swat. How she missed the girl's half-mean, half-funny way of joking. Sophie missed everyone, even her mom. She wished there was a phone she could use to call Andrea, to tell her, *Hey, I'm fine, I'm at the bottom of the sea with that mermaid, visiting some Ogresses. No, don't worry, they're nice Ogresses. Be back soon, stay away from Nana!* Sophie

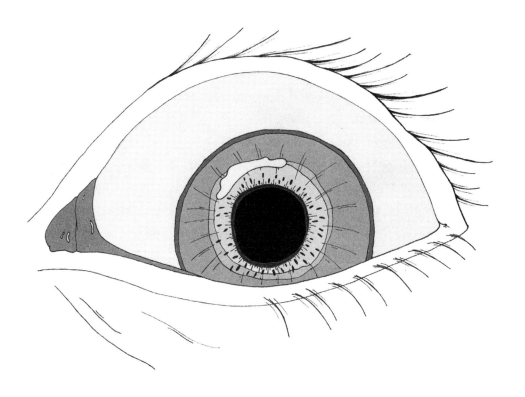

shivered with emotion. There were so many people who needed her care, but they were gone, gone for good or too far away for her to be able to help.

"Please, don't be scared." The Ogress spoke in a rich accent, her words rising high and dipping low, almost a growl—but a friendly growl, like the rumble of a curious dog. "I know we are so large, my sister and I, but we are only gentle, and we have been awaiting you. I hope you find your room comfortable."

Sophie looked around at the room. It was a cave of sorts, the walls gray and marbled, and her bed was linen stuffed with soft plants. Sophie was so exhausted she could have fallen asleep upon a coral reef, but this bed was something special.

"It's lovely. Thank you so much."

"Much better," Syrena said approvingly. "You hungry? Ogresses make you food."

Sophie's stomach rumbled at the mention of it. "I am," she said. "I don't think I've eaten in a long time. But I don't want to put you out," she said quickly. "I think I can conjure myself something."

"No, no, we fixed you a feast!" the Ogress said. "I am Fenja. My sister, Menja, would like to meet you also. We cannot both fit inside this grotto, so I will let her in now." Sophie wasn't sure but she thought the Ogress smiled as she turned around and crawled out of the cave. In a moment, a nearly identical Ogress came crawling in, her hand made into a fist the size of a boulder.

"Greetings," said Menja. "I am Menja."

"I am Sophie," Sophie said. She wriggled to sit up. Now that she was awake it felt a bit strange to be meeting these famous creatures all slumped down in bed. She patted down her tangles and hoped she looked presentable.

The Ogress brought her fist toward the girl and slowly opened her hand, revealing a stone cup of water in the center. "I thought you might be thirsty," she said.

"Oh, I am," Sophie said, though she wasn't sure that she was at all. But she was touched that the Ogress had brought her something, and it looked so funny, so tiny on Menja's giant palm. She hesitated, unsure of how to retrieve it. Would she have to scramble up the giant's fingers?

"I will get for you," Syrena said, swimming up to grab the cup of water. "Don't strain you brain." She brought the cup down to Sophie. "Is special water," the mermaid said. "Come from hole in the ocean. Much good salt. Like medicine for you."

"Thank you," Sophie said, and brought the cup to her lips. And it did taste wonderful, the salt rich, not stinging as salt sometimes is. She gulped it down.

"If you feel able, we would love for you to dine with us in our dining chamber," Menja said. "My sister and I cannot both fit in this grotto, though we thought it would make a lovely room for a human girl."

"It does!" Sophie cried. "I love it. Thank you."

"The walls are salt." The giant gestured with her fingers, running one against the wall and pulling up a spray of salt in her wake. "It's very good for you."

"I will ready her and bring to table," Syrena said to the Ogress, and the Ogress smiled, her teeth as big as window frames, and crawled back out of the cave.

"You sleep long time, almost long as in Swilkie!" Syrena told her, pulling back Sophie's bedding. "You either real lazy or need rest bad. I'm not sure."

"Syrena, I don't even remember getting here," Sophie said.

"Ogresses oooh and coo over you like sleeping baby," Syrena said, amusement in her voice. "They have this cave all fixed for you. They like to keep you forever I think! Like little girl pet."

Sophie climbed out from her bed and stretched. It felt like her body had been pummeled by a natural disaster, which, she supposed, it basically had. Her body popped and cracked as she moved. "Oh, man," she grumbled. Her hand went to her face, where the sting she got from Kishka's dragon whisker still bubbled. It was gritty with a salty ointment.

"You be fine," Syrena said. "Not like you attacked by shiver of sharks, ya? That give you something to moan and groan about! You eat from giants' feast and feel better. Wait till you see this food. Giants eat lots of food. But we must make you proper for their table. Have you seen yourself?"

Sophie looked down and took herself in. Her T-shirt looked like a wad of Kleenex, wadded up and somehow stuck to her body. Her jeans trailed more stringy bits than a jellyfish. She was a disaster.

"Syrena, I look terrible," she gasped. "My clothes are so ruined I don't even know how to get them off!"

"Is true," the mermaid nodded, and removed a knife fashioned from a sharp bit of shell from where it was tied to her arm with seaweed. She went to work cutting the girl's clothes off, nodding with her giant head of hair toward a garment laid out on a hunk of coral.

"You see that? The Ogresses make for you."

Sophie examined the garment. It was a one-piece fashioned from the same linen the giants wore, a material both hardy and soft. It was trimmed in braids of seaweed and strips of seal leather, and it fastened up the front with chalky bits of coral that fit into loops of rope. It looked like a uniform for a corps that didn't exist, a deep-sea mermaid apprentice's outfit. Sophie stepped into it and solemnly fastened the buttons. It fit her perfectly. Her hands ran down it, unbelieving; she'd never worn anything so nice. She found a set of pockets at her hips.

"Pockets!" she exclaimed. "They made pockets."

"Girl like you need pockets," Syrena said, extracting the pouch Hennie gave her from where it tangled into the belt loop of her old shorts. "Here. You keep this in pocket." The mermaid paused, giving Sophie an up-and-down appraisal. "Ya. You look much better now. Less like human girl, more like Odmieńce. Like have special task. Is good work suit."

Syrena turned on her tail, and Sophie followed her out from the mouth of a cave, swimming into an antechamber that led her into a cavern so tall she couldn't see the roof of it, just a hazy darkness. Sophie *could* see the giants' dining table, a slab of stone set upon blocks and blocks and blocks of other stones, rising like a house above her head. Glowing worms, radiating jellyfish, and glass bowls of phosphorescence lighted the room. Luminescent lantern fish swam in slow circles above the dinner table. As Sophie was taking in the scene, the most grotesque sea creature she had ever seen pulled up beside her. It was an enormous fish, its mouth cranked open to reveal a graveyard of crooked, rotting, but very sharp teeth. Painful-looking spines splintered up across its back, and a twig seemed to be growing out of its face, hanging over its mouth. On the tip of this branch was a light, glowing blue like Sophie's own talisman.

"Uh... hello," Sophie said to the fish, who seemed to be staring at her with its beady fish eyes. Sophie made an effort to look at the creature's eyes and not into its banged-up, ramped-up mouth crammed with all those teeth. Her heart pattered.

"Are you down there?" called one of the Ogresses. "We sent a fish to swim you up here. Don't be frightened! We know she can be quite surprising!"

"Just jump on her head," said the other Ogress. "Or get in her mouth."

Sophie looked at Syrena with wide, pleading eyes. "I'm sure I can just—"

"Get in the fish," Syrena hissed. "This Ogress hospitality. I meet you up there." Syrena turned and paddled up the leg of the table.

Sophie turned back to the fish, who was probably waiting patiently, though it was impossible for it not to look menacing. "Okay, then," Sophie said awkwardly. "I guess I'll just..." Head or mouth? Spiky spines or jagged jaw? "Pardon me," Sophie said, and she dog-paddled directly into the gaping mouth of the anglerfish. Sitting down on the fish's tongue, she wrapped her hands around its teeth. She felt like she was in a cage of sorts. The fish began to wiggle its fins and rise slowly, like an underwater helicopter. It was, Sophie had to admit, sort of fun. When the fish came up above the edge of the table, it brought itself to a landing before a bowl heaped with curling seaweed. Sophie gingerly swam up and over the fish's teeth and, once on her feet, gave the creature a little bow of thanks.

"That was great," she said shyly.

"Angie likes to help out however she can," said Menja, or perhaps Fenja. "She was in a some very bad relationships when she showed up here, and we helped her out of them."

"We sure did," said Fenja, or perhaps Menja. "With my very own hands I plucked three different males out of her. One had been latched onto her so long his eyes had vanished. Another had lost all of his organs."

"It's the anglerfish way," the other Ogress said with a sad shrug when she saw Sophie's surprise. "The males are parasites, they merge totally with the females—but poor Angie was really upset about it."

"They were bringing her down," the other Ogress nodded. "So we got rid of them, and now her energy is a lot lighter. She's my favorite reading lamp." The Ogress reached down and gave one of the fish's spines a little tweak. "Aren't you, Ang?"

"Not so easy on the eye," said Menja or Fenja. "But not much down here is. Wait until you see the frilled shark, if you haven't already."

"I don't think I have," Sophie said politely, waving to Angie as she swam away.

"Oh, you'd know it. Once you see a frilled shark, you never forget."

"But enough with all that," spoke the other Ogress grandly. "Please, dig in!"

Sophie was charmed by how small she was in the Ogresses' world, walking across their dining table as if she had become a fairy, or Alice in Wonderland. The table was piled high with a mountain of dried fish, crusted in banks of salt, and salted tangles of sea greens sat in chunky bowls of carved-out salt. She watched in awe as the sisters grabbed fistfuls of fish, entire schools, and tossed them into their mouths whole like they were no bigger than sardines. Sophie ran around the table like a mouse, scavenging; she sought out the occasional stray fish that fell through the Ogresses' fingers, dunking it in the dust that fell from their huge chunks of salt.

"This is *so good!*" the girl cried. It had been so long since she'd had anything but whatever raw sea creature she was able to get her hands on. To eat fish that had been salted and cured, plants that were seasoned—it was, to Sophie, the best meal of her life. She ate until her belly strained against the coral-and-rope fastening of her new clothes, and then she lay down on the table, laughing, her back against a giant jar of phosphorescent plankton, their green glow lighting her from behind. She felt overcome with gratitude for these loving giants, for Syrena, even for the anglerfish. "And these clothes you made for me. They're—so cool." Sophie looked down at herself again, gently fingering the soft strips of shark leather edging her pockets. "Thank you."

"We are so glad you enjoy it," said Fenja or Menja. The two Ogresses gazed down at Sophie, their hazel eyes catching the luminescence of the creatures swimming in the jar. "We have been waiting, like so many others, for you to come and stop the Invisible. We have watched humans descend in their submarines, trying to understand it. They are not able to stay long, and any equipment they leave gets destroyed. But they are just humans, anyway. They could only study the Invisible. They could not stop it. Only magic can stop it."

"Um... yeah," Sophie nodded, stifling a burp. She knew that in some cultures a burp was a compliment to the chef. She didn't know if this was true here, in the culture of the Sea-Ogresses. But then again, she hadn't been aware that she had a job to do here at the Ogresses'. What was this about the Invisible? She looked at Syrena, but the mermaid was busy stuffing her face, so Sophie tried to look attentive and hide her confusion.

"We have been tending the salt mill for so many years," said Menja, or Fenja. "Perhaps you can see our calluses?" She turned her palm down to Sophie, spreading her fingers. It was like looking at a topographic map, the tough hills and tender valleys running down the giant's hand.

"We're making more salt than ever now," said the other sister. "And it's not good for the ocean. The coral doesn't like it; many of the creatures don't. But the salt absorbs some of the Invisible, so we must keep making it."

The other giantess nodded, the end of her braid brushing the table and scattering fish bones onto the floor. "In fact, though we have been so excited to visit with you, it makes me nervous how long the mill has been left unattended. We get it going very quickly so that we're able to leave it for a bit as it slows down, but we always need to return. Perhaps Syrena can take you to the Invisible."

"That would be great," Sophie said, scrambling to her feet. She pretended she was not in extreme discomfort from her gorging, and she pretended she knew anything about what the giants were talking about. "I've been, like, dying to see the Invisible."

The giants exchanged looks across the table. Sophie could see the flicker of their eyelashes, wide as palm leaves. "Please, don't try to do anything heroic," said Fenja or Menja. "We know of all you've done, even the latest, when you shape-shifted into a shark! But the Invisible is far too powerful, and you still have much to learn."

"You've been a hero before and you will be a hero again, the hero of us all," smiled the other sister. "But please, keep your distance from the Invisible for now. Today you are to relax. Observe, and relax."

"Go only as close as Syrena allows," said the other Ogress. "We will see you after."

And with that, the Ogresses pushed back their chairs, stirring up

clouds of sea mud that billowed all the way up to the tabletop and settled back down in a layer of sediment. When they stood up tall inside
the cathedral of the cave, their heads became lost in the darkness of
the ceiling, and all Sophie could see of them were their long white
togas, billowing around them like undersea sails. Their footprints left
huge craters in the floor as they left, and Sophie watched as a school
of blobular fishes, their bodies like mounds of pale pudding, began flitting back and forth across the ground, refilling the craters. They had
giant lumpy noses that slid down their faces, and mouths that pulled
down in a permanent grimace. Their bodies looked like they were being
squashed by some unseen foot, their bottom halves deflating into the
seafloor, and their small, black eyes set like buttons in their chubby
cheeks. They looked profoundly upset.

"Syrena," Sophie breathed. "What are those things?"

"Blobfish, your people call them," the mermaid said. "Blobfish be
down here billions of years, before humans, before mermaids. They
born so far down the pressure crush any bone out of them till they just
blobs. Good fish, blobs. How you say, 'salt of the earth.'"

"We're really deep down here, aren't we?" Sophie asked the mermaid.

"Oh, ya," the mermaid replied. "So deep, it would normally make
us very, how you say, depressed, but for the good salt all around. Not
good to go so deep. Must be big like Ogress to handle it. Otherwise,
pressure get you. Make you cuckoo." Syrena twirled a long, elegant
finger near her temple. "Now we must go to Invisible. Is big reason
why I take you here."

SOPHIE FOLLOWED SYRENA through the labyrinth of caves that was the Ogresses' home until they were spit out into the open sea. It was darker than anything Sophie had ever seen, darker even than the dark of the mountains that rose up in the center of the Atlantic, spitting fire and birthing islands. This dark was so heavy it weighed on Sophie's eyelids. It hurt her eyes like a bright light. She squinted against it and felt a current of doom enter her heart. "Syrena," she said, "I don't like it here."

As her eyes adjusted, Sophie could begin to make out the faint glow of creatures that had been forced though the millennia to create their own light down in the depths. The gaping anglerfish, lamps growing out of their heads. The lantern fish, lit from within as if they'd all swallowed light bulbs. A grisly-jawed thing with the long body of an eel slunk by, sparks of light running across its skin like an electrical storm. A fish with a mouth like an open umbrella pulsed by, staring at Sophie with glowing red eyes. And everywhere were jellyfish, their tentacles like glowing ghosts trailing behind them. Soon it didn't seem quite as dark, not with all these creatures lighting the place up like a disco. But the other darkness, the one that had dug inside her heart, didn't go away.

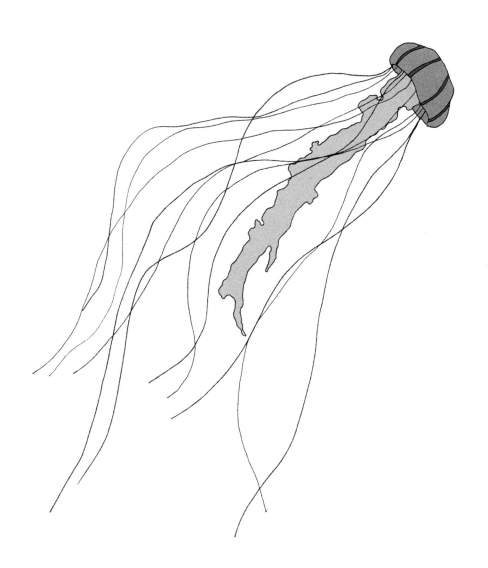

Chapter 13

"Come with me." Syrena said, and held out her hand to Sophie, who was glad to take it. Together they swam, the colorful creatures becoming sparser and sparser until again they were in blackness. Sophie knew that somewhere above her, pods of smiling minke whales glided through the water, slapping their tails joyfully. Chubby seals honked and slid their bodies onto rocks while puffins stuck their neon-orange beaks into the sea. But not down here. Though she tried to hold back her tears, Sophie couldn't help it. She let go of the mermaid's hand and started to cry.

"I'm sorry, Syrena." She faced the mermaid with embarrassment. "I just—this place is terrible."

Syrena, too, looked pained, her face taut above the dim glow of her talisman. "Is too much to be down here, outside the salt cave," she agreed. Sophie clutched her own glowing necklace, grateful that the darkness hid her crying. She was trying to be more heroic, but this horrible feeling of the deep was like nothing she'd experienced.

"Partly it is the deep, ya? It takes very long time to make light down here. Girl like you would be down here for a billion years, having baby after baby, until maybe one of them come out with a light on their head, ya? A bit of happiness."

"They're happy, the creatures?" Sophie asked. "They're not sad down here?"

"Is all they know," the mermaid shrugged. "They do okay. Making light helps. But is not just the deep, the darkness and the pressure." Syrena took a deep breath, the gills behind her ears quivering, her expression serious. "Is also the Invisible we feeling. We here now."

Sophie could barely make out the mermaid pointing into the darkness. She tried to look where Syrena was pointing, but it just looked like more nothing.

"I can't see anything," Sophie said. "Am I looking for something invisible?"

"You just wait. You be patient and watch. Is invisible, but it shows itself, too."

They hung in the dark of the deep, deep sea, an unfathomable amount of water pressing down on top of them. Sophie's mind returned to the strange shape of the blobfish, and she could feel a bit of a headache throbbing behind her eyes. What if she got crushed down here? It felt as if her spirit was already being flattened, but what about her body, her bones and her muscles? What if she turned back into the beanbag girl Syrena had had to rescue from the Boston Harbor?

As if her eyes were playing tricks on her, Sophie saw a flicker in the distance. She lifted her talisman from her chest and aimed it outward as if it were a flashlight.

"You see?" Syrena asked.

"I think I saw something," Sophie said. "Or maybe it's just my eyes getting weird in the dark." But as she kept staring, a patch of the darkness seemed to shimmer, flickering in and out of her vision. It was like a piece of glass in the blackness, but alive. Sophie could detect its upward movement.

"Is it a spring?" Sophie asked. "Is it more water, coming up from the earth?"

The mermaid shook her head, her eyes searching.

"Not is water," Syrena said. "Is something more. Feel it. Water does not feel like that."

And Sophie could feel it; when she concentrated, she could feel it hurting her heart. "Syrena," she gulped, "why are you showing this to me?"

"It is part of it, part of the bigger mystery," the mermaid said. "It have to do with Kishka. It attracted to her, the Invisible. There is legend of her down here, all the animals know her name. But recently humans start to come here, too. Scientists."

"People come all the way *down* here?" Sophie marveled.

"No, no. They send what you call, robot? Metal, thinking thing. It make picture of the Invisible. The Ogresses find one, take it apart to find out what it did. Is some kind of human tool." Syrena paused, turned to Sophie. "So you know what this is?"

"The Invisible?" Sophie shook her head, and she could feel tears coursing down her cheeks. She didn't bother to try to wipe them away. "No. I'm sorry. Maybe this means I'm not the right girl, but I don't know anything about this place."

Sophie turned her back, looking away from that creepy fountain of nothingness. She had no idea what it was, but she knew she hated it. And she knew she couldn't stay there another second. She paddled back toward the glowing creatures, feeling a wallop of gratitude at their shifting, neon colors. Syrena followed her, and in the new light, Sophie was surprised to see that the mermaid, too, was crying.

"Syrena!" Sophie gasped. She wished she could hide her surprise, but she felt so raw that she couldn't. She hadn't known the mermaid *could* cry. Like, maybe she had when she was a baby, but it seemed like whatever made tears had long since dried up like seaweed on a rock, or perhaps became calcified, coated in hardness like a pearl. A pearl. Griet. Now Sophie knew why Syrena had broken down. She reached out toward the mermaid to try to comfort her.

"Stop," the mermaid swatted at her. "I—it must be place. The deep. I miss my sister. I miss Griet." The mermaid's name came out on a choke, loosening a fresh spill of tears from Syrena's face. "Is like I never truly missed her. Never, not until now."

Feeling the mermaid's sadness, Sophie began to cry harder, her sadness for Syrena's loss mingling with that of her own. Livia, lost forever. And the others—her mother, Angel, Ella. Perhaps they were only lost for now, but down here, now was beginning to feel like forever. Finally, the two of them, mermaid and girl, wound themselves together and let loose their sorrows into one another's tangles. In this clutch they half swam, half stumbled back through the glowing creatures and into the cave of the giants.

As soon as they entered the cave, the heavy salt walls brought relief, like they were stepping from hot sun into shade. They collapsed against the nearest one and slid down into the sand, finally able to catch their breath and slow their tears, but they continued to clasp each other's hands. For Syrena, it was like holding Griet's hand once more, but of course it was also not, and so she cried a bit more. Sophie was shocked to witness the mermaid so vulnerable, and honored to bring her some comfort. She never wanted to let go of her hand; she never wanted Syrena to stop needing her closeness as she did in this moment, no matter how sad they felt. For a time they were content to simply lie there in the mouth of the cave, exhausted by what they'd been through, looking out at the flashes of creatures beyond like they were stargazing.

"Syrena, have you ever seen the stars at night, in the sky above the ocean?" Sophie asked.

Syrena had—and the memory made her cry all the harder.

"Oh, Syrena, I'm sorry," Sophie said, clutching the mermaid's other hand, bringing both of her hands up to her face like a bouquet of flowers. And at that, Syrena looked at Sophie and the flash of her eyes was like lightning in the cave and before Sophie knew what she was doing she was going into Syrena, into the mermaid's head and heart, and the mermaid was not fighting her. Inside Syrena's heart. Sophie felt a great hardness all around, *hardness, hardship, hardness, hardship,* these words looped in her head as she breathed in a wave of the mermaid's dense sadness. Griet was gone, Griet was gone forever: this knowledge was alive so deep inside the mermaid, so far down, that it felt to Sophie like she was digging, like she was getting her hands dirty, even though all she was doing was staring into Syrena's eyes while the two of them sat, perfectly still. She dug up Griet's memory, buried like something beautiful deep in the sludge, and the memory shone so brightly that it hurt, it really *hurt* Syrena as it was unearthed. As the mermaid buckled over in pain it hurt Sophie, too, and it kept hurting. Because when she pulled Griet from the mermaid's depths she pulled up other things, too, things she didn't know anything about—a winged lion with the face of an eagle reared up, roaring. A monstrous object filled the sky and dropped bombs that burned the city, made the river boil. Bodies fell on the banks. It was as if the mermaid's heart was a hive and Sophie had whacked it and out poured the bees, a thousand memories pricking and stinging: a cold so cruel the river had frozen, people staggering to and fro with blocks of ice, Syrena's fingers bleeding when she held them up before her face. Sophie batted away the images but as one was banished another surged forth. The loss was like a river, a current pushing through Sophie's heart. All the death the mermaid had seen! Something in Syrena was trying to resist her, but Sophie pushed through it, she pushed and she pulled, and she pulled all of that loss into her own heart.

The mermaid's face contorted as she pulled away from Sophie, wrapping her arms around her chest. Her fin pounded the floor of the cave, drawing a shroud of sand around them. The mermaid's gaze flashed back to Sophie, and for a moment, a weightless moment, Sophie could feel Syrena lift up inside. It was as if she were nothing, a bright, blissful nothing.

As the full weight of what she'd taken on hit her, Sophie fell back into the heavy mud of the seafloor, Syrena reaching toward her the last thing she remembered before darkness enveloped her.

IN HER DREAM, Sophie watched as a man lifted a mermaid from the water. Like a river rock taken from its home, her tail became instantly dull as the drops of seawater fell away. Her hair, lustrous and tempered by the faint blue of the sea, became lank and sticky, the tangles heavy on her head out here on land, where gravity weighed everything down. The mermaid shook her head, trying to toss her hair like she could in the water, but it just fell messily across her face. The algae that clung to her locks looked suddenly scuzzy, like mold blooming on an old plate of food. She turned back, and Sophie could see the twin fangs poking over her dry lips. When she opened her mouth, a bristle of baleen showed.

"I'll be back!" hollered Griet. "I'll be right back, please, don't cry!"

Sophie hadn't known she was crying, but when she brought her hand to her face she felt the tears. Her other hand was wrapped around something—a weapon. She tried to follow after the mermaid, but she tripped over her tail, bulky and clumsy beneath her. She opened her mouth and unleashed her zawolanie, watching as the man dropped Griet onto the rocks, bringing his hands up over his ears. The mermaid twisted, lifting herself up on her arms and turning her face to the sea.

"Stop it! Stop it! You're hurting him!" Griet shouted, alarmed. And Sophie watched as the man, his face red with pain, reached down and gruffly grabbed Griet by the tail, dragging her across the land. Sophie let her zawolanie sound again, and again the man let go of Griet, now even farther from the banks of the sea.

"Please, I just want to see how they live. He'll bring me right back!"

"Just leave her!" Sophie cried, and the man, in his madness, struck out with his boot, kicking Griet's tail, so dry now that the scales were brittle and crushed, the scars she bore from her journey standing out in stark relief. Griet cried out, ducking her head, and the man lifted her tail again and dragged her away, and Sophie could do nothing more than watch them go. Her eyes locked with her sister's as she was tugged away across the earth, her face turned back to her home.

Chapter 14

Sophie awoke choking on her zawolanie like it was caught in her throat. With a burning sputter she swallowed it back down. As she came to her senses, she found that she was looking into the pale, bulbous face of a giant octopus. A tentacle, slinky and long, was curved around her brow; she could feel the slight tingle of its cups across her skin. Another tentacle lay on her chest, across her heart. She followed the outstretched arms of the many-armed beast and traced them to Syrena, lying beside her. The octopus cupped the mermaid's head as well, and lay upon her breast.

"Is it working?" A voice emanated from a long swath of linen that rose like a curtain toward the ceiling. Somewhere high in the darkness, the Ogress spoke. The octopus didn't respond, but bobbed its head. Beneath its translucent skin Sophie could see pulses of light.

"Yes," Syrena murmured. "Is working. I see her, now. I see everything."

Sophie felt a strange relief as the octopus massaged her. It was like she was a sheet of ice cracking apart beneath something warm, turning first to slush and then to a liquid peace. The octopus withdrew its tentacles gently, twining them together in a bundle and settling onto the floor where Sophie and the mermaid lay.

"You took my *heart*," Syrena said, turning to the girl. "You took too much. It was not, what you think, the curse, the Invisible, whatever you seek to remove. Was my *heart*. *My* heart."

"But you were so sad," Sophie said. "There was so much of it. It was beautiful, and all mucky, all buried so deep, it was hard for me to get to—"

"It wasn't for you," the mermaid snapped. "Is *mine*. My Griet, and my Griffin. My wars, my beloveds, my Krystyna. You took them all and I was empty. And that was even more terrible."

"But it's supposed to feel good," Sophie protested weakly. "I was trying to help you. You were so sad."

"Is okay to feel sad. Sadness okay. Your sister get taken away by spoiled prince, okay to be sad. Your love become dead from your very own weapon? Okay for sadness. Your, what you call, bestie, best human friend become shot by bullets till not breathing? Your city set to fire? Your home, your river, torn to pieces? The people you supposed to protect dying right at your banks, with you no help to them? Make you very sad. If not, you monster. Do not make me monster. I am mermaid. I have mermaid strong heart, hold many sad things. Is built for such."

"I'm sorry," Sophie whispered. She felt as dry as Griet upon the banks, everything alive in her curling up. She shuddered at the memory and wished she could give it all back to Syrena, every last bit of it, even this last haze of it upon her heart.

"If I grow to hatred because of Griet taken from me," Syrena explained. "If I never love after Griffin slayed. If I never fight again. If I give up on humans after they kill one another at my banks, make my river into graveyard. That you take. You take the hate and the pain that makes more hate and the pain, that brings madness. But sadness? Sadness is innocent, like salt, like pearl. Like Griet. You leave me with my sadness."

With a gust of wind, the Ogress bent down to look at Sophie. Her enormous eye was full of feeling. "You are doing such complicated work, Sophia," she whispered. The breath of her voice blew across the girl like weather, a warm salt breeze. "Fenja and I, we tried to fix it, too. We thought we could grind goodness into the world, to outweigh the bad. But it didn't work. The Invisible only had more to prey upon. So we began to mill the salt, and that works some. It absorbs the Invisible, we know it does. But that, too, upsets the balance. The sea, it should not be so salty. But it's the best we can do. You, you're like a surgeon."

"Ya," Syrena nodded her head. "Is true."

"You must learn to go in and take only the bad. There are many sadnesses that may *feel* bad, but they have to stay. The heart cannot function without them."

"Why can't I just take it all?" Sophie cried. "I hate that Syrena feels so bad!" She turned to her friend. "I hate that you feel like that," she said, and her eyes filled with tears. When the mermaid smiled upon her so kindly, the tears came forward, spilling down the girl's cheeks.

"You may have taken some bad things, ya? Bad I did not know I had. I do feel lighter. But when you take away all the sadness, I so disoriented, so lost. Heart is compass. Love help me move forward every day." Syrena looked upon Sophie, and with a gasp inside her heart the girl realized that the mermaid loved her. In her tough, mermaid way, Syrena loved Sophie. "You help me, Sophie," she said. "Griet help me, her memory. Love and sadness, together. Must not take the sadness that love holds."

Sophie nodded. All she had taken from the mermaid left a residue like a fog around her heart. Bloody sunflowers. Muddy cubes of ice melting on the bank of a river. "What was all that?" she choked.

"It my life, Sophie. And I will tell you all, as I have been. But is my life. Okay?"

"Yes," Sophie nodded.

"Syrena will teach you how to tell the good from the bad," Menja told her. For such a booming whisper, it still soothed. "It's all part of your training."

"I your guinea pig, yes?" Syrena asked. "You experiment on me like mad doctor!"

Sophie peered deeper at the mermaid. "Syrena, I really do think I helped you. You seem happier. I think I got something."

"Okay, so what. Broken clock right twice a day, ya?" The mermaid giggled.

The octopus, quiet on the floor, undulated toward Menja's foot and slithered its tentacles across it, tapping.

"Sophie," said the giantess, and straightened back up to the ceiling, her long braid hanging down her back, making waves as it swung. "The Vulcan would like to work with you. It has some things to show you."

The octopus slid off the giant's foot and swam back to Sophie.

"Vulcan amazing," Syrena affirmed. "Bring me back my heart. Has big powers, for healing and for seeing. Thank you." The mermaid held up her hands, flat, and the Vulcan tapped against it with his tentacles. "If I have eight hands I give you all for high five," she said. She swam away, toward the giantess. "Now I leave you alone," she said.

SOPHIE FACED THE octopus. It was a mysterious, slightly ghoulish figure. Its skin was so pale it glowed like an apparition. And it glowed for real, too, with little pulses of light here and there, visible through its translucent skin. Its legs swayed gently, like little scarves in a wind, the tips curling and looping. And its head! Bulbous, slightly cone-shaped, its eyes on either side of its long head. It was very different from the small creature that had been living in her hair for the past few days. Sophie reached up to check that it was still there, and her fingers felt its tiny tentacles, raised in greeting. The Vulcan extended the thinnest tip of an arm as if to shake hands with it. Then it placed that arm on Sophie's head, and then another arm, and then another. And then all of the Vulcan's appendages were cradling Sophie's head, and she was

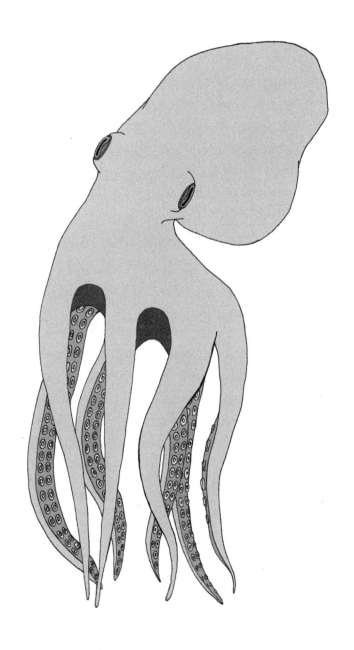

looking into its flickering face. She tried to fearlessly face the strange and groping creature, but it was hard. Its eyes were splayed so far apart, and it seemed to be looking directly into her heart.

The Vulcan tipped itself back, and Sophie was looking at its underside, where a ferocious little beak curved out from the center. She couldn't help it—her heart skipped. Was this where it would end? After all that she'd been through, now she was to be eaten by a giant octopus in the den of an Ogress? Fed to him, practically, by the creatures she'd trusted? Sophie took a deep breath, summoning her powers. She would zawolanie this stupid Vulcan or whatever it was to smithereens, send it smashing through the roof of the cave, feed it to the *Invisible!* She had battled Kishka, and won! She would not be done in by this leggy bottom dweller!

As if sensing her fear, one of the Ogresses piped up. "The Vulcan," she boomed gently, "Is an oracle. A deep-sea shaman. Not only a healer, but a seer. It can transfer energies—move thoughts and feelings from one creature to another. That is how it helped Syrena, and you, too—it took the emotions and memories you'd taken from her, and returned them. So now Syrena is whole again, and you are relieved of the burden of her history."

Thank you, Sophie began to address the octopus, but as she began to speak, the Vulcan's beak opened, and out from it came a bubble.

The bubble floated, wobbling, toward Sophie, and what she saw made her words catch in her throat. It was Hennie, her magical aunt. As if she was peering into a snow globe, Sophie watched as the old woman rocked a child in a giant wooden rocker, a storybook spread on her ample lap. Sophie recognized the toddler, though she had never seen her so animated, poking at the book with excited fingers, laughing up at Hennie's face, her sweet and jowly face, tugging at the babushka knot beneath her chin.

"That's the Dola's baby," Sophie gasped. "I mean, Laurie LeClair's." And as the bubble spun in the water before Sophie, she saw a figure hunched over a desk, scratching into a notebook. Dark roots grew out from the top of her head, fading to bleachy white and spilling over a pile of books. The figure raised her head and glanced in Hennie's direction, and a smile came over her face like a sunrise. It *was* Laurie LeClair. And she no longer had the look of the Dola, that dead-eyed creature, nor the dead eyes Sophie had seen blinking from Laurie's face when she'd seen her wasted in the square so many times, either. Laurie's eyes were as fiery and alive as her baby's, as glinting and happy as Hennie's. They were helping each other, Sophie understood, and it was good.

As the bubble popped in front of her, the Vulcan opened its beak and released another.

Dr. Chen stood at her rooftop dovecote. Sophie could see all of Chelsea in the bubble's round distance—the green stretch of the Tobin Bridge carrying cars into Boston. The red-and-white water tower rising cheerfully from the Soldier's Home, the veteran's hospital on the hill. It looked like a sweet toy town from this angle. But Sophie noticed that the dovecote was empty, and that Dr. Chen's smooth face held sadness and worry. Stray feathers caught in the structure's mesh were fluttering in the wind and Sophie reached for her hair, finding Livia's feather snared tightly in the tangle. Where were the pigeons? Sophie bit her lip, watching the doctor pull the feathers free from the wire of the dovecote, creating a small, fluffy bouquet. And as the tears fell from her gentle face, Dr. Chen lifted all that was left of her flock and dried her face with the soft clutch.

The image popped, leaving Sophie with an anxious feeling that only grew when she saw what lay inside the next wobbly orb. It was a green bubble, blown from the Vulcan's curved beak. Green with a thickness of plant life, with crawling vines and leaves like elephant ears, floppy and prehistoric. Then a hand rose up like a pale flower and pulled the greenery down, and Sophie was looking at herself. Herself with well-kept, untangled hair pinned back neatly with a barrette. Herself with smooth skin, pale skin, skin that had never seen sunlight, had never had a sunburn, let alone felt the searing lash of a sea dragon. Herself with eyes empty of struggle, empty of conflict, empty of concern, or of thought. Her own eyes, empty. Staring back at her.

Inside the bubble, Sophie's sister raised her hand as if she could see Sophie watching. Sophie raised her hand as well, a reflex. She raised her right hand to the girl's left, tilted her head left to her sister's tilting right. Could her sister see her? The pale girl's eyes remained empty, almost cold. Tiny tree frogs, colorful and venomous, hopped around her from leaf to leaf, onto her shoulders and off. A desperate feeling stirred in Sophie's chest. She didn't even know her *name*. Her own sister. She opened her mouth anyway. "Hello?" she cried, and her

twin's eyes widened, her mouth hung open.

"Help me!" Sophie's twin begged, in a voice that sounded as old and creaking as a jammed attic door. The effort of the words on the girl's dry throat produced a spasm of coughing, which drove tears from her eyes. Sophie brought her hand to her mouth, covering it in horror. *Help her?*

"Can you see me?" Sophie begged. "Who—what—what's your name?"

The girl coughed, and coughed, and coughed, until a thick green liquid curled out from the corner of her lips. She tore a leaf from a plant and mopped her mouth.

The name *Belinda* floated through Sophie's body, feeling like an itch, like the beginning of a cold. The name felt bad inside her, and she too began to cough, as if she could hack it from her lungs. *Belinda.* It drifted through her, leaving a poisonous trail. Sophie imagined the red bumps of a rash, but inside her.

"Belinda?" The word left Sophie like the croak of a frog, not the nimble ones that leapt across her sister but a bullfrog, something warty and bulbous and stuck in the mud. Her sister's big eyes searched her jungle home, looking for something. *Belinda*: the word had left a residue in Sophie's throat. She coughed it out and the burst of air from her lips shattered the bubble into a dozen tinier bubbles, each containing her sister's white face, then each shimmered into nothing, gone.

"No!" Sophie cried, distraught, pawing at the empty space in front of her, as if she could whip the bubble back from the sea itself. "No, I wasn't done! I heard her!" Above her the giantesses' faces loomed like statues of stone, stern and sad. Syrena's face, smaller and closer, looked just as tight.

The next bubble left the Vulcan's mouth like a puff of smoke. It was Andrea, her mother, sitting by a window in the house Sophie had left behind. A chipped plate was balanced on the windowsill, and Andrea absently flicked her cigarette ash onto it. Her mother had gone back to smoking! Sophie felt a tug in her heart. She'd like to pull the thing right from her mother's melancholy grip. She'd known her mother used to smoke, back when she was young and wild. She'd quit when she became pregnant with Sophie and her twin sister and abandoned Ronald, their father. When Ronald fell under Kishka's spell at the dump, plied with endless alcohol, alive but dead, the closest thing to a zombie Sophie hoped she'd ever see. And Sophie knew, as she watched her mother, that Andrea was thinking about

Ronald as well. Sophie could feel it. She was thinking about Ronald, and she was thinking about Sophie. In her cocoon of smoke, Andrea was waiting, and thinking of the people she had lost.

Sophie watched as her mother stubbed the cigarette out on the dinner plate, and went to place the plate on the wooden back stairs. As her hands reached through the window her arms seized as if she was being electrocuted and the plate jerked from her hand, rolling onto the back porch. Andrea's face twisted in pain; she tried to bring her arms back through the window, into the house, but they appeared to be stuck to the air itself.

"No!" Sophie cried helplessly. "No, no!"

With a terrible grimace of effort, Andrea managed to yank her arms back inside, the strain knocking her on her back on the kitchen floor. She clambered up, shaking tears of hurt and fear from the corners of her eyes.

"Goddammit!" she hollered into the empty house. She hugged her arms together, rubbing her elbows. She swiped at her eyes, wiping her tears back into her frazzled hair. She struck out at the kitchen table, which Sophie saw was piled with a great tumble of long boxes. They crashed to the floor and Sophie could see what they were. Cigarettes. Cartons and cartons of cigarettes. Andrea kicked at them wildly and raged through the house, to the front door that led out to Heard Street. She dove for the knob and was flung back from the door as if a terrible shock had struck her.

Andrea ran back through the house, into the kitchen, stomping the boxes of cigarettes beneath her bare feet. She reached out for the back door that led out to the stairs, and Sophie flinched in advance, covering her eyes so that she didn't have to see her mother shoved back by the force field that was keeping her hostage in her own home.

"Please!" she heard her mother demand. "Please! Let me go!"

When there was quiet, Sophie dared to peek again. Her mother was back at the window, a new dinner plate beside her, dusted with ash, a torn-open pack of cigarettes on the sill. Andrea inhaled the cigarette, shaking. She blew a smoke ring toward Sophie, and the bubble popped.

"No," Sophie said, turning to the Vulcan, her voice a pleading echo of her mother's. "Please. I don't think I can see any more." But the Vulcan exhaled its next bubble, and Sophie couldn't look away.

It was Ella, alone in her room. She lay facedown on her bed and, from the look of her heaving body, she was crying. Her hair streamed out in all directions, black and lustrous, a shine that could light the deep, Sophie thought. She missed her friend with a sharp pang. What was hurting her? Sophie feared the sight of Ella pulling herself up from her bed and revealing her lovely face abraded, scrubbed compulsively with a rough sponge or a chemical meant for dirty pans. Sophie's heart ached for her friend. Could she get inside her, somehow, and take that thing away, the thing that made Ella feel so dirty she thought she needed to scour herself that way?

But maybe Ella wasn't even hurting like that anymore. Maybe her dumb new boyfriend had helped her stop; maybe the need to be pretty for him was bigger even than her need to feel clean. Maybe she was crying because he'd hurt her, in her heart or, Sophie thought, her body.

What if Ella rose to reveal a black eye, a cut lip? Sophie's heart curled into a fist at the thought of it. She would turn into a shark again. She would swim back to Massachusetts and find the boy at Revere Beach; in the scummy froth she'd swallow him whole.

But when Ella rose up, her face was the same lovely face she'd always had. No imagined germs had been sanded off her cheeks, and no harm had come to her eyes, muddied with eyeliner and tears. Her lips were not split, though they trembled. Sophie spied a crumple of pink upon her best friend's lap; she'd been folded over it, lying upon it. A dented cardboard box and a sheet of unfolded paper. Sophie could see instructions, diagrams. Illustration of ladies' fingers holding some sort of stick. And there was the stick itself, pink and white plastic on Ella's pink bedspread, bright pink strips in the tiny plastic window. Sophie suddenly understood what was wrong. Ella was pregnant.

The bubble whooshed away before Sophie could call out.

She turned to the Vulcan. If she hadn't been so afraid of the clawlike curve of its mighty beak she might have pressed her hand against it, made him swallow whatever was coming next. "No more," Sophie told the creature, covering her eyes. The Vulcan's many tentacles rubbed her head, relaxing her, and eventually she took a deep breath and wearily opened her eyes. In the bubble wobbling before her was Angel. Her heart leapt with love and fear—what would Angel be doing? Was she okay? She was bent over, her strong arms in motion, her longish-shortish hair swaying at her chin. Angel was... doing dishes. Sophie laughed a large, joyous laugh—to see something so boring! Angel wasn't fighting Kishka or crying or stuck somewhere she didn't want to be. She was finishing the last of the dinner dishes, there in the home where she lived with her mother, the *Curandera*. She was tucking a knitted afghan around her mother, who was watching a Spanish soap opera in front of a flickering television. She was walking into her bedroom and pulling from her dresser the clothes she'd wear tomorrow, a button-up shirt and a pair of jeans. She was placing them on a chair in her bedroom, getting ready for bed. Oh, it was all so mundane, Sophie's pent-up tears sprung with joy. Imagine! Just to be home, washing milk from a cereal bowl in the sink. Settling into the tired couch to watch reruns with her mom. The sort of comfort Sophie hadn't recognized as comfort when she was just a normal girl. Maybe it had even bored her. From her new position on the ocean floor, a psychic octopus's tentacles wrapped around her head, boredom suddenly seemed nice to Sophie.

The Vulcan was done. It removed its arms and brought them low around its body and they undulated close to the floor, levitating the creature slightly. Sophie's head tingled and her heart felt full. Battered, but hopeful. At least Angel was okay. And Ella, she hadn't hurt herself. Her mother—it was impossible to find a silver lining in what she had seen her mother going through. The memory made her blood chill. And her sister. She had seen her sister, and her sister had seen her. She had learned her name—Belinda. She yearned to see her again. Even though it hurt and frightened her, to see this strange, twisted version of herself, she longed to speak to her again. Belinda needed her help.

Such a strong mix of fear and sadness and love swirled through

Sophie, and she thought, *This is what I took from Syrena.* How terrible it would feel to have these emotions taken from her! Would she rather not have her love at all? Of course not. Sophie realized how wise and magic the Vulcan truly was. As much as it had shown her, it had revealed so much more: the makeup of her own heavy heart. Sophie reached out and clasped two of its curling tentacles and brought them to her face, kissed them.

"Thank you," she said quietly. She could already feel it pulling away, beginning its weird ghostly swim back into the depths. It patted her cheek briefly with one slender tentacle, then drifted deep into the cave and away.

That night, alone in the Ogresses' cave, her head snug on a firm pillow of kelp, Sophie thought of her people, far away in Chelsea. How could she help them from so far away? She felt happiness at the thought of healthy Laurie LeClair, of baby Alize gurgling on Hennie's lap. She took comfort in *their* comfort, as if it were she mundanely studying for a test under the supportive eyes of her aunt. She wished! Her sister, Belinda, was still a mystery. Her mother was trapped, but there seemed to be little Sophie could do to help her. Maybe she could send in Angel to help, but that would be basically feeding Angel to Kishka. Maybe she could handle it, but Sophie wouldn't risk it. She had to trust that Andrea was Kishka's daughter, had been dealing with her evil since before Sophie was even born, and would be okay.

But Ella. Sophie remembered the vision of her friend, alone in her room, crying. Ella, Angel could help. With Sophie gone, Ella needed someone, anyone to tell her problem to. She'd never tell her mother or any of her aunts. Poor Ella, surrounded by people but feeling so horribly alone. If Sophie were there she would do anything her friend wanted, anything to help her. Ella needed someone like that, not just a friend but a *best* friend, someone to listen to her and hug her and light her cigarettes and help her do whatever she wanted to do.

Sophie grew quiet inside herself, became still and went very, very deep. She sunk into herself like she had sunk into the ocean around her. She could feel the support of the salt in the water, the hum of it coming off the walls of the room. In the thin shaft of light her talisman created she watched as the tiniest motes of salt streamed around her. She reached out for Livia's feather and stroked it gently. And then she sought Angel.

THOUSANDS OF MILES above her and thousands more across the land, Sophie sought her friend's heart, and she found it, bursting into the familiar space with too much speed, too much gusto, too much excitement. She could feel Angel's gasp rush up around her, Angel's instinctive push to raise her walls, but Sophie had already breached them, and she was strong enough to keep them down. She filled Angel's heart with her essence, and Angel, back in Chelsea, her back against a bench in Bellingham Square, became filled with wonder.

Sophie?

Yes! Sophie's energy raised, was pure yes, and Angel was filled with laughter, her hands held to her heart as if she could feel her friend there, her eyes wide with delight. "Oh my god, oh my god!" She said aloud, joyful laughter spilling from her mouth, attracting the attention of some elderly ladies sitting nearby as well as a cluster of teenagers hanging on the corner—"Angel be *tripping*."

Angel collected herself. The bus with its bold yellow stripe slid up to the curb, accordioned its doors open with a hiss to welcome the ladies and the teens, then crinkled shut. Momentarily alone in the busy square, Angel whispered, "Sophie?"

Sophie buzzed a scolding *Ssssssshhh!* into Angel's heart. They didn't need to use real words, and Angel didn't need to call attention to herself. She could just sit there on the bench and feel what Sophie had to tell her.

Oh, it felt so good to be in Angel's heart again! She couldn't help but peek around a bit. She saw her friend hard at work, taking tests, talking to people, and she felt how these people recognized Angel's goodness. She saw Angel at a desk, talking to teenagers not much younger then she was. She felt the way Angel held them in her heart as they cried. Sophie was impressed. She couldn't do that. Those teens were the ones who had shouted to her on the streets, forced her to take different routes home, sped by on dirt bikes, hurling catcalls in their wake. Sophie didn't have room for them in her heart, but Angel did.

She tried to talk to Angel but found that the words didn't work, not in long sentences. They got lost, fizzled out, or arrived in Angel's heart slightly off, like a psychic version of the telephone game. She picked big, strong words, and sent them one at a time, like flares. *Ella. Pregnant. Help.* She conjured the image she'd seen in the bubble, of her friend hunched over the pregnancy test, sobbing. She made sure Angel saw the little plastic strip with the terrible pink lines, Ella's face swollen and pink with tears. She felt Angel wrap her heart around the scene, as if giving it a hug. Sophie felt the squeeze in her own heart, and it brought tears to her eyes. Angel understood. Sophie was filled with gratitude. Her link to Angel was so strong, and Angel's own powers so excellent, that they could communicate like this, across worlds.

Even with her message delivered, Sophie didn't want to leave the familiar space of Angel's heart. She could feel her friend wanting to know everything. But where could Sophie begin? She could send the words *Ogress, Cave, Deep Sea,* and hope for the best. But maybe such words would alarm Angel? They *did* sound kind of scary, if you didn't know better. And Angel didn't. She didn't know anything. Sophie was overwhelmed by the weight of her story.

There was no way to tell it like this. So instead she opened up her heart in a bubble of love. *I'm good.* She hoped the phrase would land in Angel's heart with all the happy vibes she'd packed it with. She could feel Angel's response, one of relief and gratitude and an itch to know more, but Sophie had no more to give. The time spent traversing space and time to leap into Angel had exhausted her, even in this room of salt. She blew a kiss, and like a rubber band she shot out from Angel and back into herself.

Back in Chelsea, Angel felt the vacancy with the same shock as the girl's arrival, and was glad she was sitting down. *Whoa.* She touched her heart again, and it was empty of all but herself. Her grin as the bus pulled up was big enough to eat the whole city. Sophie was okay! She was keeping tabs on all of them, somehow. And she needed a favor. Angel was happy to oblige. She strode onto the bus and took her seat, gazing out the scratched and spotted window, watching the city pass by. The world was amazing, bigger than she could ever fully know. She would find Sophie's friend and see what she could do to help.

Thousands of miles beneath the sea, in the Ogresses' ancient castle, Sophie slept hard, soaking in salt through the night.

Chapter 15

"**T**his has been quite a difficult stop for you," said Fenja from the edge of the Swilkie. It was morning, and Sophie and Syrena had feasted one last time at the giantesses' giant table. It was time to move on.

The Swilkie's eye was narrow at the mill, the gargantuan contraption the Ogresses cranked and spun, bringing salt into the sea. It was little more than a dust devil in the water. Sophie and Syrena would swim up alongside it and, as it widened, enter the tunnel easily, swimming through its center to the surface.

"We knew it could be hard, just entering the Swilkie, and beholding the Invisible. But we didn't expect there would be so much hard learning," said Menja sadly.

"Is no problem," Syrena said. "Is even good. Lesson must be learned, what better than here, in Ogresses' cave? You take good care of us both."

"Yes," Sophie chimed in. "Thank you so much. It has been an honor to meet you."

"The honor is ours," said Fenja. "We hope you enjoy the Jottnars' party. We so wish we could join, but—the milling." Fenja sighed an Ogress sigh, a blast of air that rose to the surface, creating a rogue wave somewhere in the middle of the ocean.

"Party?" Sophie gasped. "We're going to a party?"

"Oh, ya," Syrena nodded. "And I truly need one at this point, ya? Don't you?"

Sophie hadn't really thought about it. The last party she'd gone to had been Ella's birthday, back in the spring. Ella's whole family had been there, and they sang a birthday song to her in Spanish. One of her uncles had a drum that looked like a tambourine, and he smacked it to keep the beat. They ate *mofongo* and *tostones* and *flan*. And Ella got a million presents, a big jumble on her kitchen table, a pile of shiny paper trash and ribbon on the floor. Sophie had bummed money off her mother for a month leading up to the party, slowly collecting enough to buy Ella a T-shirt at the decal shop at the mall. BEST FRIENDS read the decal Sophie selected, with two glittery butterflies flying off together. She got her best friend's name on the back in velvety pink letters. ELLA. Sophie had hoped that when her birthday rolled around, Ella would buy the same shirt for her, with her own name, SOPHIE, spelled across the back. But by the time Sophie's birthday rolled around, who knew where she'd even be? Were she and Ella even friends anymore? She thought about the image of her friend crying in the Vulcan's bubble. *Pregnant.*

If Ella ever needed her best friend, it was now. And where was Sophie? A million miles beneath the sea, hanging out with blobfish and giants.

"Oh, I should know you be, how you call it, party-pooper," Syrena grumbled, giving Sophie a poke.

"When you exit the Swilkie, you'll find a dolphin pod waiting for you," Fenja said. "We've arranged for them to ferry you to Laeso Island. That's where you're headed to, yes?"

"That's where the party is," Syrena said in what sounded like a chirp. Sophie had never seen her so buoyant.

"The dolphins have some things for you," Menja said. "Some gifts from us."

"You've already done so much," Syrena said, smiling.

"Yeah, really," Sophie chimed in.

"What you are doing for us, both of you, is beyond anything we could do for you," Menja said. "Sophia, we have been tending this mill since we were children. Just kidnapped slaves. The king had mistaken us for grown women, but we were just babies. And we worked his mill, slowly growing into our Ogress selves. Eventually we grew large enough to banish the king, but then we understood how close to the Invisible we were. It's probably what made the king so terrible! And so we continue to mill the salt. Perhaps after you're done with your duties, perhaps my sister and I can take a break! Or mill something else. Who knows?"

"It's nice to think about," Fenja said dreamily.

"I would hug you and kiss you," Syrena said, "but would be awkward. You both so big."

"Sending you big, crushing giant hugs!" Menja boomed.

And Sophie and Syrena swam up along the Swilkie, and as it widened, swam easily into the eye.

"Getting in is easy," Syrena said. "Leaving is hard."

"Am I going to get caught in the whirlpool again?" Sophie worried aloud. After all she had been through, her resolve to not be a whiny teenager, to behave in a way more fitting to a half-Odmieńce, was forgotten in the face of the Swilkie.

"Not unless you screw it up," Syrena said. "Must leap out! Like dolphin. Or like mermaid."

"Leap out?"

"Ya," Syrena nodded. "Come up to the surface fast and strong. Explode from surface! Like rocket, ya? Leap into the air! Leap away from the Swilkie. No problem."

"Ya," Sophie said, in an unfriendly mockery of the mermaid's voice. "Just 'leap.' No big deal."

"Do not do that, Sophie," Syrena snapped. "Too cheap for magic girl."

"Sorry," Sophie mumbled. She had mocked Syrena, but really she had only envy and respect for the mermaid. They had grown even closer down here in the Ogresses' world, and all Sophie wanted was to be as confident as Syrena, as worldly—or underworldly. Ocean-y? She wanted to believe she could leap out from the Swilkie, easy and elegant as a flying fish skimming the ocean surface. Even a giant, cumbersome whale could break the surface with grace.

That thought gave Sophie an idea. She had morphed into a shark to defeat her grandmother, so why couldn't she morph into a sea creature to dive out from the Swilkie? Why couldn't she become a whale? Or even a mermaid?

I could! Sophie thought, a marvelous thought. *I could become a mermaid!* Her powers intimidated her, and some of them truly scared her. She didn't quite understand how she had become the shark, but she knew it had to do with desperation, and fear and anger, powerful emotions that fused with her magic. She wasn't angry at the Swilkie, and she wasn't terrified, not like she was of her grandmother. But she was definitely scared.

Swimming behind the mermaid, the water under her command, Sophie watched the way Syrena's tail writhed and kicked. It undulated elegantly, but with the force of something shot from a cannon. Sophie imagined her lower body moving in such a way. She mimicked the mermaid's motions, as much as she could in her human body. Above them the sea's surface was a sheet of glittering blue, framed by the dense froth of the Swilkie. *Like jumping through a hoop*, Sophie thought. A flaming hoop. What if she missed it and belly flopped into the Swilkie? Well, the water would seize her and spin her and make her its puppet. She'd twirl for days, weeks, months, until Syrena broke the spell or grew bored and went on to her party. No, she couldn't let it get her again. Sophie kicked her legs like pistons, watching as Syrena burst through the surface, her body arcing in the air above her, casting a sparkling shadow above the water. And then it was Sophie's turn.

The zawolanie that left her mouth created its own miniature storm inside the whirlpool. Sophie saw the water change as the sound hit it, creating a path for her to follow out and over the Swilkie. The sound of the zawolanie as she broke the surface was an unearthly siren; it rang in Sophie's own ears, briefly, and then she was up and over, plunging back into the sea. She had done it. She had made it out.

ABOVE THE WAVES, Syrena's mouth hung open as if ready to sing her own curse. Around them bobbed a pool of dolphins, some wearing packs, like burros, some outfitted with reins of seaweed and linen. All of them were decorated with large chunks of salt, and all of them were looking directly at Sophie.

Eeeeeee iiieeee eieieie, one sounded to Syrena. The mermaid looked confused and a little offended at the noise, and turned back and forth between the creature and Sophie.

"Well, you were correct, there is only one mermaid!" Syrena barked at the dolphin. "And it is I!"

The pod looked at Syrena, and then returned their gaze to Sophie. Where she once had legs, she now had tails— two solid fishtails covered in a mosaic of scales, ending in flukes where her feet had been. Sophie's own eyes widened at the sight of herself. She lifted her new tails and gathered them in her arms, laughter pouring from her mouth. She inspected her scales, glinting like a chain mail of new jewels. She gazed at her twin flukes, the delicate webbing at the scalloped tips, and rubbed them against her face.

"Oh, come now!" Syrena hollered. "What is this, love festival? That nice, you help yourself out of Swilkie with magic, very smart. Now—" the mermaid clapped her hands together—"back to girl, please. We must go to party."

"But Syrena—*look*!" Sophie swam toward the mermaid—swam! Like a mermaid! She tilted her hips and her tails gently propelled her through the water. "Check it *out*! I'm a mermaid!" She brought her hands, full of tail, up to Syrena's furrowed brow.

"No, you *not* mermaid. You Odmieńce making magic. Now, come on. Back to normal."

Sophie could not *believe* she'd just been coasting through the sea—for how long? It felt like ages! Coasting through the sea on a boring current of water when she could have been *mermaiding* through the water with her twin tails! She gathered her hair behind her and did a triple flip, rolling over and over, her tails muscular and gleaming. When she came to a stop she was dizzy and giggling. Suddenly it wasn't a big deal to have a head full of tangles. She was not an unkempt girl—she was a *mermaid*.

"Sophie, no," Syrena said. "Is not good. Can't stay in shifted shape for so long. Is moment-magic." She cleared her throat, and soberly swam over to Sophie's tails, running her fingers along scales. "Very nice job, though." She relented. "Very nice, the double tail. Make sense for human girl."

"Odmieńce girl," Sophie said proudly, conjuring a haughty confidence.

"Oh, please," Syrena scoffed. "Odmieńce girl. Enough, now. Dolphins await. Expecting girl and mermaid. You confuse them."

"I'm going to stay like this," Sophie declared.

Syrena shook her head sternly. "Over my dead mermaid body."

"You're not the boss of me, Syrena," Sophie said. Jeez, weren't they just *in love* with each other down at the Ogress cave? Now they were back to their bickering. Maybe if Sophie were Syrena's equal, a mermaid too, things would be smoother between them.

"I sort of boss of you," Syrena said, her eyes glinting. "This my world, down here. You my charge."

"But if I'm a mermaid it's my world, too. We can both be the boss."

Syrena snorted with frustration, tiny glinting bubbles trailing out from her nostrils like a sea-bull. "Sophie! You not mermaid. You in your magic now, and I tell you, not good. Not good to be in magic for so long."

"Which way to the party?" Sophie asked Syrena.

"We go when you girl again."

Sophie turned to the pod of dolphins. "Which way to Laeso Island?"

The dolphins answered in a peal of unintelligible squeaks.

"God! Well, I guess I'll just figure it out on my own!" And Sophie took off.

Her speed took her own breath away. With her two tails, how fast she could cut through the waters! She turned only to make sure the rest of her party had not been blown away by her powerful wake, but there was Syrena just behind her, followed by the pod of dolphins, frolicking as they traveled, as dolphins will.

"Wrong way," Syrena said grimly, pulling up alongside Sophie and grabbing her by a fin. "This way." The mermaid made a sharp turn, practically slapping Sophie with her tail. Sophie, too, made a quick swerve and was soon on the path to Laeso.

Syrena swam just ahead of the girl-mermaid, and no matter how hard Sophie worked the waters she could not catch up with her. *Fine,* she thought. *Show off. Syrena's been in the water for hundreds of years. I think I'm doing pretty awesome for my first day as a mermaid.*

Breaking from the pod, a single dolphin shot ahead to swim beside Sophie. Its head was covered in an intricately braided harness fashioned from seaweed, and giant chunks of salt were threaded through the headdress like beads. Sophie slowed for a moment and gave the creature a warm smile, reaching out to pet its flank. It was smooth, smooth like Syrena's skin. The creature was darker gray on top, fading to white at the front of its body and to a dusky light gray at the back. In the center, the colors met in a dip like an hourglass. Sophie traced the pattern lightly, smiling. The creature's dark eye met hers and its chittering beak opened.

"Hello, Sophie." It was not the undecipherable trill of a dolphin. It was the flat monotone of the Dola.

"No!" Sophie wailed, in exactly the voice she kept trying not to use. She used it again. "No!" She kicked her tails like a baby mermaid having a tantrum. Up ahead, Syrena turned around to see what was the matter. A glimpse at the dolphin told her everything. She broke out into a smile so big you could see her baleen.

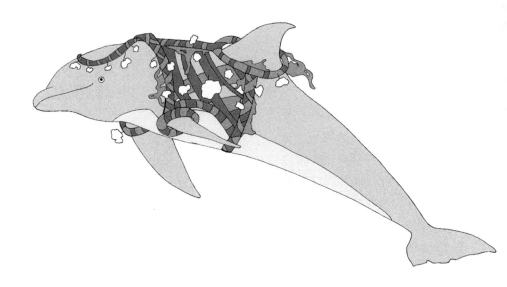

"Dola! *Tak dobre cie widziec!*" The mermaid waved her hand above her head in a happy hello.

"This isn't fair," Sophie said, the fight already half gone from her. She had debated with the Dola before, when she had turned her back on the wisdom and kindness of her Aunt Hennie, when she had used her magic in the service of her own stubborn self, instead of what it was meant to serve. But what was that, even? *Humanity*? The *world*?

"*Nie mój problem.*" The Dola spoke Polish through the dolphin's mouth, the flat, monotonous sound of its voice giving Sophie instant creeps.

"Give me a break!" Sophie pleaded with the dolphin Dola. "I have to do all this horrible, hard work, and I get all these amazing powers and I can't even have a little *fun* with them? This is totally not fair."

The Dola shrugged its dorsal fin. "No such thing as 'fair.' Only what is, and what is not. You are not to use your shape-shifting like this. Not for such prolonged period of time. It's not good for your body. You are not meant to do it."

"And yet here I am, doing it!" Sophie yelled. "God, don't you get tired of these arguments?"

"Yes, always," the Dola replied calmly. Even the calm and acquiescent timbre of its voice made Sophie want to die. It was like nails on the chalkboard of her soul.

"You have a tremendous gift, this ability to shape-shift. And it is tremendously taxing on your body, on your magic."

"But I feel *great*," Sophie insisted, and did a mermaid leap to prove her point, breaking the water's surface and gracefully returning, slapping at the waves with her lush flukes for effect.

"Yes, you are doing very well here in the ocean. But you're getting a constant salt infusion. Being with the Ogresses healed you, and the salt at Laeso Island is particularly replenishing. But you will not be down here forever. You must conserve your energy. There will be a time of recovery, and it will be hard on you. Don't make it harder."

"And what if I don't?" Sophie sulked, but she already knew the answer.

"I will stay beside you until you obey me or become mad from my presence," the dolphin Dola said.

"I bet I can outswim you."

"I will hop into whatever vessel I need to. Shark, fish, octopus. Dolphin. Syrena."

"You wouldn't take over Syrena!"

"I will do whatever I must. And Syrena understands. She would let me occupy her. She cares about you. She does not want you doing this."

"She just wants to be the only mermaid," Sophie said. "She's just mad that I can become like her in a snap."

"She thinks you act like a child," the Dola said, "and you do. It is her job to protect you, and she takes it seriously. Now become yourself again and I will carry you to Laeso."

"I'd rather you just go away," Sophie said. "I'll make my own way to the island."

"I am traveling there, too," the Dola explained. "I have a meeting with Ran about a ship."

"Who is Ran?"

If a dolphin or a Dola could make an expression of surprise, the dolphin Dola would have shot such a look at Sophie.

"You do not know Ran? You are going to her island."

"I don't know anything," Sophie said. "Because Syrena doesn't tell me anything."

"Yes. Because you act like a child. It is hard for her to level with you. To treat you as equal. You should act different."

"I *know*," Sophie said. "I keep trying and it doesn't work."

"It will," said the Dola. "It is your destiny to grow up. To become mature."

"And it's not my destiny to be a mermaid for a while?" the girl asked, with just a little bit of begging at the edge of her voice.

"Nope. So, become a girl again and hop on the dolphin's back, please."

With a zawolanie that sounded like the loudest, worst, most annoyed and petulant sigh ever uttered by a teenager, Sophie sulked her tails away and was a girl again. Her legs felt bare and naked in the cold water, ungainly and ungraceful. Their kicks were goofy, as if she were trying to find the pedals to an invisible bike.

Syrena was beside her. "Ride the dolphin."

"It's not a dolphin, it's the Dola."

"Either way. Will take you. Relax. Fun to ride dolphin!"

"More fun to be a mermaid."

"And you were." Syrena looked deeply at Sophie. "You were a mermaid for a moment. How magic for you. How many girl want to be mermaid, huh? And for moment, you feel it."

"My legs feel dumb now."

"Ya. No help down here." Syrena reached out and slapped Sophie's legs good-naturedly. "It almost sweet," she said, "to have another to swim with. Not swim with another mermaid since Griet. I wish it could be allowed, Sophie. But law is law, is bigger than me."

"Is it bigger than you, Dola?" Sophie kicked her heels into the dolphin's flank, like a cowgirl on an ornery horse.

"Of course. I don't write destiny. I only enforce it."

"Don't you enjoy the Dola?" Syrena smiled.

"No, not at all! Doesn't its voice just go right through you?"

The mermaid shrugged. "Not so much. I think it worse if it you she come for."

"How do you two even know each other? Do you just end up meeting everyone if you live for hundreds of years?"

"Dola very close with Ran, who run island we going to. And Ran take me in when I was young. After losing Griet. I had nowhere to go, and Ran and her daughters very kind to me. Dola come often to sink ships."

"Figures. You're like the Grim Reaper or something."

"Actually, Ran is more of the Grim Reaper," the Dola interjected. "I just tell her what needs to happen. She carries it out."

"So we're on our way to a party at the home of some lady who sinks ships?"

"It sounds awful when you say it like that," Syrena said. "You just no understand all."

"Do you?" Sophie asked. "Do you understand it all?"

"I understand my part," the mermaid said. "And you should make more effort to understand yours."

"She will," the dolphin Dola predicted, the words escaping its smiling beak in a trail of tiny bubbles that shimmered like silver sequins.

Chapter 16

For a while Syrena stayed, alone, ducking along the rocky shore of Kattegat Bay. It was not easy, and it was not safe. When the story of the captured mermaid spread through the village, many townspeople came to the banks for a glimpse of the second one, the one who stayed in the water, screaming a terrible scream as her sister was carried away by the prince. *Carried away*. It sounded romantic, the way the people spoke of it, but they hadn't been there. Syrena had been there, had watched her sister being dragged along the ground by the man, like a stag he had killed in the woods and was bringing home for supper.

Children and mothers often came to the banks of the Kattegat. The children patted the surface of the water with their tiny, chubby hands, and the mothers scanned the depths with fear and excitement. They didn't really believe that mermaids stole babies, but who could be sure? Courting couples came to steal a glimpse of the creature, and if they were lucky a kiss as well. Old fishermen, bitter at the catches these creatures had stolen from their boats, hung around smoking tobacco and waiting to give the mermaid a piece of their minds. Old women came, for a peek at the beast, they said, but really to claim a moment's peace along the rocky shore, breathing in the salty night air. The presence of mermaids, in the town and in the bay, had shaken up the villagers' daily routines. Who could be expected to stick to their ironwork or roofing or washing or cooking when such legendary creatures were near? It gave the town a feeling of a festival, a carnival.

Another group came to the bay, too, clambering into boats and searching beyond the shallows for the prince's mermaid's sister. Young men, unmarried and unattached, harboring the ambitions of a prince despite their lowly status as shopkeepers, or blacksmiths, or fish curers. They had seen the drawings of the prince's mermaid in the newspaper, with her cascading hair and pearly teeth popping over her pouty lips. And that tail! It was said that the prince kept her in a great glass tub so that her tail would shine and her hair become soft, and that soon he would marry her. The king and queen were upset, of course, that their son hadn't selected a neighboring royal, for it was no benefit to their land to bring a mermaid into court; indeed, the superstitious among them whispered that such an act would anger the sea gods. To them, the occasional howls from the creature in the bay, as haunting as a nightmare, seemed a grim portent.

Staying close to the seafloor, Syrena could look up and see the hulls of the men's boats sliding by overhead, hear the men calling for her in great, drunken cries. As awful as a single man could be, a pack of them was more awful still. Syrena hugged her narwhal horn, wondering what good it was if it couldn't bring back her sister. How she wished she could storm the land! She would weave a lasso of shark teeth and bind the prince with the flick of her wrist. She would not be a merciful avenger, oh no! She would spit on the prince as the shark teeth bit into him. With her sister on one shoulder and her horn held in the other she would slay whoever stood between her and the sea. Griet on her back, she would haul them both into deeper waters and they would sound their siren calls below the waves and rejoin their family. Surely, the warring must be over by now.

"Here, fishy, fishy, fishy!" the boys called out from their boats. Like a stargazer fish, Syrena dug a trench with her tail and burrowed into the sand, her face peeking out to observe the motion of the vessels.

"Marry me, mermaid!" the boys shouted. "No, me!" they shouted. "No, me!" "Me!" "Me!"

Syrena knew that it was only a matter of time before one of these ruffians tumbled from his boat. Their slurs grew thicker, and their bumbling movements echoed down to Syrena's hiding place. And when it happened, Syrena did not feel the cruel glee she imagined she would feel. She felt annoyed. Deeply, thoroughly annoyed.

So much for being an avenging sea beastess, she scolded herself as she flung off the mud and swam up to where the boy kicked desperately, his soaked boots and knickers weighing him down. The cacophony of his helpless mates was an additional annoyance. Humans were such fools. They had barely a moment on earth, and they wasted it drinking poison and behaving terribly to everything. How easy it would be to pull this one down by his foot, to drag him into the depths with her. *You'd like to marry a mermaid, would you?* She would bare her fangs. *Well, I've been looking for a husband to live down here with me.* But Syrena couldn't do it. It was not her way.

Syrena did seize the boy's leg, and a newly hysterical sound burst from his mouth. She brought him beneath the waves, dodging the desperate swats and grabs of his hands, his frightened kicking. "Don't panic!" Syrena yelled at him. Despite the roar of his struggle, he heard her. "Panicking is the fastest way to drown. Surely, a sailor like you must know that!"

The boy became still in the water, staring at the mermaid with widened eyes. He could not see her as well as she could see him, but he knew what she was. And now he knew that the story was true, that the Mermaid Princess did have a sister in the waters, and he quickly understood that she was not at all interested in a human husband.

"You tell that prince of yours that if he does not return my sister the whole of the mermaid queendom will go to war upon your village. We will wipe you out as if you never existed. We will take your pine, your deer; we will tell the fish to abandon your bay. You will starve, and your homes will be nothing more than charred, smoking stumps. Do you hear me?"

With one fist Syrena gripped the young sailor by his collar; with her other she clutched her narwhal horn, poking it into the boy's soft throat. Unable to speak, conserving his breath, the boy could only nod—but nod he did, jerking his head in urgent, trembling motions, his eyes huge to show her he saw her, he understood her. He brought his hands together in a gesture of prayer and she released him, flinging him to the surface, where he broke the water with a hoarse gasp of terror and relief. Syrena darted away, swimming all the way to the outskirts of the bay, far from the men and their ships. She would pass a day here, allowing the word of her threat to spread. Then she would return to the banks to rescue her sister.

Far out in the bay, the mermaid lay upon her back, floating on the sweet little waves on the bay's surface, gazing up at the sky full of stars. Weren't these things supposed to grant wishes? Syrena wished upon each one—*Griet, Griet, Griet.* The hope in her chest grew heavier with every plea, and she let herself sink beneath the waters. Perhaps the stars only granted the wishes of humans.

"I REMEMBER ALL this as if it was yesterday," the Dola said. Sophie's octopus had scurried down from her head and was now splayed across the dolphin's bulbous brow like another festive decoration.

"Did you go to Syrena then?" Sophie asked the creature. "Had she acted against her destiny?"

"Not at all," the Dola said smoothly. It was true that since Sophie had obeyed her destiny, the Dola's voice did not weigh so heavily upon her soul. "It was meant to be, all that happened to Griet and to Syrena."

"Well, it sounds terrible," Sophie said quickly, glancing at Syrena. She would never get used to how insensitive the Dola was. Syrena had lost her sister, and the Dola shrugged it off like it was just another day on earth.

"Is okay." Syrena reached out and patted Sophie. "I accustomed to Dola. And everything so long ago."

"But it's in you still," Sophie said. "I felt it."

"In me like my bones, girl," the mermaid smiled.

"It's just not okay," Sophie insisted. "None of what happened is okay."

"You right, is not okay," the mermaid agreed. "But still meant to happen."

"Was it the work of Kishka?" Sophie asked, and Syrena nodded slowly.

"In part, yes. The prince had evil in his heart. He had been hurt, too, very young. And so his hurt turned to that darkness that Kishka feeds upon. She grow very strong from men like prince. And men like him grow strong from Kishka."

"Like mutually beneficial parasites," the Dola suggested.

"Well, I don't see any benefit!" Sophie snapped, and gently bonked the dolphin on the head. She lifted her octopus and nestled him back in her tangle. She'd become accustomed to the small weight of him on her head and felt strange without him. She turned back to Syrena, flying through the water beside her.

"Then what happened?"

"Well, you know, all the things I say to sailor, they mostly lies. There no mermaid queendom. We all split apart. No one to help anyone anymore. But I mean what I say, also. Feel like could burn down his village. Me, a baby mermaid, can't go onto land, even! Me, to destroy village! But I feel I could." The mermaid touched her heart.

"I want to burn down their village, too!" Sophie said hotly. "So they didn't bring Griet back to you?"

"They did," Syrena said sadly. "They did."

THE SPUTTERING SAILOR had gotten his audience with the prince, though it pained the man to allow the bug-eyed, hysterical man trembling into his chambers. The sight of him gave the prince shudders and he brought his hand—clad in the softest leather from the softest baby lamb ever to have been born in the village—across the sailor's face in a bracing slap.

"Get it together, man!" the prince barked. "Unless you want to spend the rest of your days chained in a basement with the rest of the village's madfolk. Compose yourself."

With a huff and a puff that brought tears from his eyes, the boy tried to settle his breathing and conjure up a bit of dignity. An audience with the prince, inside his very chambers! If he lived past this, if he was not carried off in chains or slayed by a pack of brutal sea witches he would have a marvelous story to tell!

Shaking, he bowed deeply at the waist. "Your highness," he spoke, directing his voice down at the polished wood floor.

"Speak up—what is it?" The prince was becoming impatient.

"Your highness," the sailor stood upright and looked the man in the eye. "I came upon your... the... your Mermaid Princess, your highness. She has a sister. Quite terrible and strong. I came upon her in the bay."

"Did you?" the prince sounded unimpressed. Perhaps he did not believe the boy.

"Truly I did!" the sailor swore. "You must believe me, sir! She pulled me under—I thought that she would spear me! She carried a big... a sharp—"

"A type of horn, was it?" The prince recalled, squinting upward, where the wainscoting trimmed his quarters, where swags of silk hung decoratively. "Like one stolen from the brow of a unicorn?" He smirked and raised an eyebrow.

"No—well, yes, your highness, it was—"

The prince came forward and clapped the boy on the back, nearly knocking him over. "You are truly in a state, lad!"

He pushed the boy a touch harder, until he fell backward onto a tufted chair. "I am toying with you, and it is most unkind of me. Allow me to apologize." He walked to a cabinet, and from a great hollow crystal poured a stream of clear liquid into a glass. He passed it to the boy. "That will steel you. Drink up."

The sailor did as the prince commanded, choking as the liquid, which looked like nothing more than a gulp of water, burned its way down his throat. He was familiar with ale and the other brews the peasants fermented in their wooden barrels, but what the prince drank was far more powerful. Already dizzy, the boy imagined it was the juice of the crystal itself. He tried to gather his wits. "Your highness, she warned of a great war if you do not return her sister to the sea. She predicted destruction, such fearful destruction! Our whole village, gone! The fish called away! Famine and fire! A race of sea witches descending upon our town!"

"You were right to come to me," the prince said. "I must always know of any threat to our land, no matter how weak it may be."

"But your highness, she is not weak, I promise you!"

"Not weak to a drunken boy who had tumbled from his boat," the prince allowed. "Am I right? You were clumsy and foolish that night, were you not?"

The sailor hung his head. "I was," he admitted, ashamed.

"I too have seen this beast," the prince said casually. "An ugly thing. But they're all ugly, these sea witches." He knocked back his own glass of crystal liquid and poured the boy another.

"Trust me, boy. They have their magics. Beneath the water, they shimmer. But you bring them upon the land and—they're useless."

"Useless, your highness?"

"They lose their luster entirely. Their hair, for example. It becomes brittle as straw. I gave her to my maidens, told them to oil her hair, and—nothing. She is brought back to me with her hair dry as kindling, and green, all coated in oil." The prince shuddered at the recollection. "A very painful sight."

"Y-yes," the boy nodded, sipping the terrible drink. "It must have been."

"And the tail!" the prince exclaimed. "Marvelous in the waters, to be sure. But take a fish out of the water, and what do you have?" He tilted his empty glass toward the boy and stared at him hard. His eyes, the boy realized, seemed to be the same color as the drink. The color of no color at all.

"A fish?" the boy offered hesitantly.

The prince snorted a great snort of laughter. "Take a fish out of the water and yes, boy, what you have is a big, stinking fish. And who wants a big, stinking fish stinking up his home, eh? Not even a fisherman wants to live with his catch! And certainly not a prince!"

The prince sat down in the chair opposite the boy and rubbed his flaxen head in his hands. He leaned back in his seat, his pale face made red from the stress of his story. His hands clutched the decorative fish carved onto the throne's wooden arms.

"I gave her to my personal fisherman," he recalled. "You must— everyone must understand that I did my best. I sent my doctor to her as well. Is she a fish, is she a girl—well, the mystery of it all becomes quite tedious when she's rotting away in your bathtub, I tell you!"

"Certainly, your highness," mumbled the boy, feeling chill.

"I said, get rid of the fish of her, and return her to me as a woman! I can't have that smell in my palace, and I can't have a bride that can't dance! They can't dance, boy! I hadn't thought of that when I grabbed her from the shore. That a woman would need legs to dance, proper girl legs. What sort of bride is a bride that can't dance with her husband on her wedding day? And what kind of queen cannot walk among her people? I ask you, boy. What sort of queen smells like rotting fish and can't dance?"

"Surely no sort of queen for you, your highness," the boy said numbly, his mind reeling at the story. He remembered the iron grip of the mermaid's sister. If he brought his hand to his throat he could feel the rough spot where her sword had scratched his skin.

"Ah, it's all no good," the prince sighed, rising from his seat. "She came back from the fisherman even worse than before. My doctor swears he did his best, but he'd never worked on a mermaid; it was a terrible mess, just awful. No one's fault, of course—"

"Of course," the boy said quietly.

"She still can't walk, and now she can't seem to swim either. She's ruined. So fine, go, take her back to her sister in the bay. Maybe she can do something with her."

"She—she's here?" The boy stumbled to his feet and felt the blood rush from his face down to his feet. He swayed with the drink and the prince's words. He watched, rooted to the spot, as the prince pulled back the long curtain that obscured his private bath. There, alone in the large stone tub, lay the Mermaid Princess. It was true that her hair was green; it tumbled down onto the floor, where it bunched on the tiles like a heap of moss. Her skin was nearly green as well, a pale, pale green, and in the dim light it looked even more sickly, mottled with splotches of pink and yellow. Her eyes were closed and her quick breaths sounded like wind through dry grass. Her full lips were cracked and white.

In his horror at the sight of the mermaid, the sailor forgot the power of the man he addressed. "Your highness, but—she's your princess, your highness. You were to marry her, were you not? Maybe if you were good to her, her sister will not bring a war—"

"Oh, fear not." The prince swatted his hand, glittering with rings, at the boy, sweeping away his concern. "There will be no war from that wench. She's alone out there. They have no nation, mermaids. They are odd fish, solitary swimmers." The prince regarded the boy. "I thought you came to collect this thing, bring it back to the bay? Was I wrong?"

"No, your highness, I was delivering the mermaid's message. I would have taken the princess back to the bay, but—"

"But now that you see what's become of her you're afraid the sea witch will have your head? Is that it?"

The boy swallowed. There were so many things to be afraid of— the powerful prince, the vicious mermaid, the wan princess, grisly in the bath. "Yes, your highness."

"She gave you a good scare, I know. But she can't harm you. Stupid things can't manage outside of the sea. Go on," he motioned the boy toward the bath. "I can't keep her in here another moment. Can't you smell her?"

The boy nodded his head. He could indeed smell the Mermaid Princess. The smell of gutted fish, and something saltier. The smell of tears.

"Take her!" The prince had lost his patience with the lot of it. "Bring her back to the bay, leave her there for the sister. I don't want to see her again. And you, if I see you again, if I hear of you again, babbling about a war, I'll have you chained up with the other idiots. You understand?"

"Yes, your highness."

THE BOY'S WALK to the bay took him from the castle down the village's main road, lined with shops and cottages, houses that opened into public kitchens, ateliers where artisans brought boughs from the woods and fashioned them into things useful and handsome. Alehouses, a school, a church. His walk took him through the heart of the village, and as he walked, the truth slid quick as fire through every building, and the villagers knew that the rumor had been true.

The prince had taken the beautiful creature and turned her into a monster. What he had tried wasn't right for any human, not even a nobleman. The rumor had spread, whispered from house to house, that the fisherman who had made the first cut did so through a veil of tears. That the doctor had been threatened with death if he refused. And so as the fisherman had cut, the doctor had stitched. They worked together, both men weeping, their ears stuffed with cotton and wax so as not to be driven mad by the cries of the mermaid.

The villagers stood in their doorways as the boy walked past in a funeral parade of one. They clutched the things that were holy to them—woven branches or the shed antler of a stag, a precious stone or lock of hair. They prayed to their goddess that she be forgiving, show mercy to the villagers who lived under the rule of a man who would do such a thing. They asked that she bless the dirt the Mermaid Princess bled upon. They begged that she forgive the doctor and the fisherman. They prayed even that she forgive the prince, though none of them were certain they could do the same. To be as forgiving as a goddess: what powerful and mysterious being could have created them all, the simple villagers and the innocent sea girl and the monstrous prince? They could never understand her ways, but still they lit candles and let them burn into the morning. They scattered salt in the streets and in the corners of their homes, hoping to bring purity. But many of them felt that they would never again know such a thing as purity after watching the boy pass them by, his face covered in salt and tears, the dead mermaid in his arms, her terrible legs made of stitching and scales dangling, swaying against his own, her tangled green hair dragging in the dirt.

When the boy reached the shore, he got to work. The long walk through the village had fortified and sobered him. He no longer felt the icy-hot liquor of the prince, nor the chill of the man's colorless eyes upon him. He felt the strength and soul of his village in his heart, the presence of all who had come out to bear witness to the great tragedy. He could feel them with him as he marched. He could feel the warmth of their candles; he could feel the pain in their eyes; he could feel their strength in his chest, where his heart thumped. He knew it was as a village that they would return the mermaid to her sister, though he alone would face her.

With his bare hands the boy peeled sheets of bark from the trees that lined the shore. He laid them out, one on top of another, pounding flat their curl with stones. He scoured the shore for the sharpest rock he could find and cut holes around the edges of the bark. He gathered fistfuls of seaweed and laced them through the holes, tying them tightly. Then he laid the mermaid princess on the raft, covering her body with a swath of her long hair, already softened by being closer to the sea. Tenderly he curled her horrible patchwork legs beneath her. Scales scraped off into his hand, and he sprinkled the dust into the sea. What was once a tail, fat and healthy, had been sawed in half; the devastation of the tools upon the mermaid's flesh was visible, the scaled skin red and swollen with infection.

Looking away, the boy tore young boughs from the tree and covered the mermaid with great and leafy branches; he piled them upon her body until she was obscured, the terrible legs hidden. Her head lay upon her great bundle of hair as if on a pillow.

And then the boy lifted the raft, bringing the mermaid to the edge of the farthest rock, the one that jutted deep into the bay; he placed her upon the water, and with a gentle push he returned her to her home.

His fists, when he brought them to his face, smelled of her. It was not the rank smell the prince had complained of. It was the scent of the sea itself. Salty and sweet. The smell of birth and the smell of death. He caught his tears in his fists and wiped them on his pants. He watched the mermaid move deeper into the bay until he could no longer see her. The sun had set, and the water was darkness.

Chapter 17

"**H**ow strange," Syrena said, her voice soft, almost mesmerized. "How strange to be here, now. At this point in our story."

The travelers floated a mile or so away from what appeared to be a great golden glow emanating from the waters. It was as if the sea turned to honey, lit with the dancing of a hundred thousand bees. Such a glittering vision—the opposite, thought Sophie, of the Invisible. The light called to her, called to them all, dancing luminous inside their eyes. Even the Dola looked more soulful as it gazed in the direction of Laeso Island.

"Isn't it interesting," the Dola spoke, "how long our stories are? That now, so many years later, it would still seem as if it were only just beginning."

The mermaid looked at the Dola with tears in her eyes.

"I come here," Syrena said to Sophie, and paused, collecting her thoughts. Her tears were a delicate blue, lighter than the blue of the sea, like a bit of sky falling into the ocean. "I come here after I lose Griet."

"Did you... did you see her when they brought her back?" Sophie asked, though she wasn't sure she wanted to know the answer.

Syrena shook her head. The glow of Laeso Island lit the tears like gems suspended in the water. Sophie wished she could reach out, take one, and slide it into her pocket, or weave it into her hair with Livia's feather.

"I did not want to see. The silver fish, they come to me. They wrap me in a cloud, spinning and spinning around me. They tell me what happen to my sister." She shook her head, and her tears swirled like miniature Swilkies. "I could not see her like that. I—I frightened, to have such picture in my head. Perhaps coward. But I could not. I summon dolphin to visit the boy, to tell him I will not come for him. He try. He show respect to Griet."

"But Griet," Sophie said urgently. "She—she just, she sank, and..."

"She return to the ocean," Syrena said simply. "She fall to the sand, she feed the creatures. Like every creature in the sea. We pass away, we fall to the bottom. We feed the creatures. The creatures, they pass on, feed more creatures. Always been such. Since beginning of earth, beginning of sea."

Sophie nodded. It seemed sad to her that there wasn't anything to commemorate Griet's life. A stone at the bottom of the sea, a piece of coral, something she could visit. It was silly, she knew. Griet was gone, and Sophie had never known her. But still.

She could feel Syrena reading her feelings in her gentle, mermaid way. "You are beside her," Syrena said. "She all around us. She the water, she the fish. Griet, the sand in our hair. Bless her."

"Bless her," Sophie echoed in a whisper.

"I so lost after she gone," Syrena said. "I did not know where to be, where to go. When we were together, anywhere we travel good, because we together. Anyplace we travel the right place. Without her, was like I did not know direction anymore. I swim in circles. Sharks come close, they see I have a sickness about me. They wait for me to be weaker and weaker. But then, I see light." Syrena pointed toward the golden mirage. "Ran and her daughters come for me. They hear my story, traveling before me on the fishes. They come for me and bring me back to their cave beneath the island. And I live with them for many years. Like family."

"Are they mermaids too?" Sophie asked.

"They are Jottnar, magic people. Like Odmieńce. They live in sea and earth. Very, very old. Not giant like Ogresses, but bigger people. Very strong. Can do most anything. Big muscle, big hearts."

And as if she had summoned them with her praise, two women were suddenly upon them in the water, one embracing Syrena, the other grabbing Sophie by her hips, surging her forward at a great, wild speed.

"Whoa!" Sophie hollered, her mouth filling with water. "Whoa, there!" Being hugged by a Jottnar was like being carried on a powerful current. The woman's hands, large as Sophie's head, gripped her waist, but the woman did not seem to move. It was if they were flying.

Beside her, Syrena and the other woman tumbled in circles, like puppies. They hugged and rolled and their laughter flew past Sophie's head in big bubbles.

"I am Bara!" Sophie heard the woman introduce herself, shouting into her ear. "Daughter of Ran and Aegir! That's Unnr, my sister! We couldn't wait, it's been taking you forever to get here!" Alongside them the dolphins leapt and dove through the wakes they generated. Even the Dola seemed to be having fun. Sophie burst out laughing.

"Aren't they fun!" Syrena called as she swirled by. "The Billow Maidens! Oh, Sophie—it is so good to be here. Unnr, that's Sophie!"

Unnr, who Sophie sometimes saw as a lovely, strong woman with tumbling hair and sometimes saw as the surge of the current that carried them, howled a *hello* at the girl.

"We know all about you," Bara shouted from behind. "Famous Sophia!" Her voice was teasing, but not unkind. With a final surge the current shoved them through the mouth of the cave, where they came to a short stop in a kind of grotto, sputtering and splashing. Syrena, still tumbling, bumped her head against the cave's wall, coming to a stop.

"Oh!" she cried. "Pesky maiden! Lucky I have much hair to save my noggin!" Unnr rose from the water with the mermaid in her arms, twisting with happiness, spinning Syrena to and fro, her great tail flapping wildly. Bara was much gentler with Sophie, bringing her to a stop that sent up a spray of water onto a raised stone where an assembly of very tall, very attractive people looked at them.

"Mother!" Unnr turned toward the gathering and held Syrena out as if she were a child. "Look what I found!"

"Be careful with dear Syrena!" cried a woman with long silver hair. She wore a crown of spiraling shells around her brow, and her dress seemed to be made of water itself, shifting and spilling over her like the most elegant Grecian toga. "And hello." She addressed Sophie with a kind and crinkled face. "You are Sophia. We have great party planned for you. I hope you are ready."

"Party," Sophie repeated dumbly, the word making her realize how tired she was, like even her bones were exhausted. She would maybe like a *sleeping* party. Maybe even a party where she'd sleep so deep she'd wake up back in Chelsea with a normal family. Normal, non-evil grandmother. Normal, cranky mom. Normal boy-crazed bestie. Pigeons that didn't talk, creeks free of mermaids.

But even as she had this thought, this familiar wish, she realized it didn't quite sit with her anymore. The thought of giving up Syrena was impossible now. And to have not known Livia? To have not known Livia would be worse than having lost her. Sophie truly understood the sadness that Syrena kept so close to her heart, the loss that she cherished. Sophie had such a loss, too.

"Meet my daughters," Ran said. "Bara and Unnr, my waves. So strong, are they not? Strong and happy. Hard workers."

She turned to another girl, with wet sticky hair, crimson and heavy. She did not look happy like Bara and Unrr. "Blooughadda," Ran said.

"My right-hand maiden. Mother's helper. Not very happy, no. But so strong. Say hello, Bloo."

Bloo bared her teeth at Sophie and waved one hand idly. Her fingers were topped with sticky red nails.

"H-hi," Sophie stuttered.

"Dufa," Ran continued, motioning to a giggling girl who seemed, Sophie thought, a bit drunk. She swayed this way and that, so simple and happy that Sophie thought she was perhaps not all there, that she had a child's mind in the body of a great, gorgeous woman.

"Dufa!" Syrena cheered at the sight of her.

"Hel-hellooooo," Dufa cried in a high-pitched voice, giggling at her own tipsy gait.

Sophie turned to Syrena and whispered, "Is she—is she drunk?"

"Drunk on the tossing of the great sea!" Dufa hiccupped cheerfully. "Drunk on the drinking of great whirlpools spinning down my gullet!"

"Sophie!" Syrena snapped. "Is—how you say?—rude to talk about people as if they are not there! Especially Jottnar!"

"I'm sorry," Sophie said to the woman, who bowed at the waist as if in curtsy, then began to topple.

"I'm Hefrig." Another maiden stomped toward Sophie and, crouching down upon a rock, bent to offer a crushing hand for shaking. Sophie hesitantly lifted her hand in return, and found it swallowed up to her elbow by Hefrig's mighty grasp. "I sent my sisters for you," she said. "And I've been helping Papa with the feast, boiling the ale and the fish. It's not so often we get company, you know. We couldn't be happier. Syrena is like one of us, and one of Syrena's is one of ours as well."

"Thank you," Sophie said.

"My turn!" shouted another maiden, who swam over to Sophie and wrapped her fully in a hug, twining her arms and legs around the girl. The sensation reminded Sophie of being at the beach with her mom, before she'd learned to swim. Revere Beach in summer, the smell of coconut tanning oil and the spray of the surf, her little-girl arms and legs wrapped tight around Andrea, who held her safe, bobbed her in the water. This was how the maiden had embraced Sophie. Except the maiden was three times larger than Sophie, who was close to smothered by her clutching.

"Hronn!" a voice Sophie could not see hollered. "*Goddess!* Get it together!"

"A girl!" Hronn squeaked, intensifying her hold on Sophie. "A real, human girl! Oh, I love you! I love you so!" And then the maiden Hronn was tugged away by a final maiden who looked upon both Hronn and Sophie with such disdain the waters turned chilly and Sophie's teeth began to chatter.

"This is Kolga," Ran said proudly. "Like all my daughters, she serves her purpose."

"To family!" hollered a man, mostly obscured by the passel of females. He nudged his way through, a crown of coral rocky upon his head, a beard as unruly as Syrena's hair tangling from his chin.

A wide shell overflowing with ale sloshed in his palm, and with a wink at Sophie he dumped it into his mouth.

"To family!" Syrena cheered, and all the voices followed, a roar of sound that echoed in Sophie's ears.

"I'm Aegir," he bellowed, "and this is my family."

"We're *your* family, are we?" Ran said. The lift of her eyebrow created a ripple of water. "I'd say you're *our* family!" Everyone laughed, but Sophie felt a little left out, a little homesick for her own faraway family.

Syrena swam over and grabbed her hand. "Listen, was impossible to prepare you, they are so wild, ya? But you will grow used to them. They wonderful. Let us go with them. I stay close to you, ya?"

But Syrena did not stay close in the endless caverns. As they moved deeper into the cave that was the Jottnar palace, rooms led onto rooms, all decorated with gleaming golden artwork and sculpture, with long wooden tables set with china and crystal. Treasure chests spilled with gold and rubies, for nothing but show it seemed. Sophie's mouth nearly watered at the sight of it. Strands of pearls and hunks of emerald, diamonds that caught the light and stung her eyes. All of it pure decoration here under the sea.

In the largest room, all manner of creatures frolicked beneath a vaulted cathedral ceiling. Dolphins chittered and fish flopped and spun. The Billow Maidens danced, making waves that pulled and tugged Sophie this way and that. Anxiously, Sophie waited for Syrena to return, but the mermaid was glowing, deep in conversation first with Aegir and then Ran, then falling into the fawning clutches of Hronn, who covered her with kisses. Sophie spun in the currents and gazed at them all. The Jottnar were uniformly beautiful, with thick hair and clothing made of water. Shells and coral decorated their hair, too, but not in the sloppy way they hung in Syrena's locks—the Jottnar wore fishbone tiaras and barrettes of barnacles studded with pearl. They draped themselves casually in the spoils of the treasure trunks, layering golden webs upon their bodies, then tossing them away. Even Aegir had a thin strand of diamonds bunching his long beard midway down his belly.

Sophie had never seen Syrena so joyful. The mermaid tilted her head back and laughed. The Billow Maidens played with her hair, braiding it and tying it into knots and bows, decorating it with lengths of pearls pulled from the treasure chests as if they were nothing more than a Tupperware craft box. Golden platters were piled high with food, crabs and lobsters and fish of all sorts. Even the dolphins were part of the party, chomping the seafood right from the platters.

Sophie was able to pick the Dola out from the pod. Still heavily decorated, a bit apart from the others, not partaking of the Jottnar feast. *The Dola looks like me,* Sophie thought. *The Dola doesn't belong down here, and neither do I.* Sophie imagined what Ella would say about this place. She would be bored, with all these girls and not even one boy to get giddy about. She would say funny, mean things about the Billow Maidens, and probably pocket some jewels from the treasure chests. Sophie was suddenly gripped by a longing for her friend that was so great it felt like her heart had hiccupped. She should bring her back a trinket, a souvenir. What would Ella want? Sophie rummaged through the great chest, picking through golden coins and diamond crowns. Maybe she should bring her two souvenirs, Sophie thought—one to pawn for all the money it could bring her, and one to keep for herself.

Sophie felt Kolga approach before she saw her. The water turned suddenly cold, like bathwater that had been sitting for hours. Sophie shivered and turned, and there she was. Her eyes were blue, as were her lips, and even her skin seemed like she wore grayish blush on her cheeks. Still, she was beautiful. She smirked at Sophie.

"You like our jewels, do you?" she said in a chilly voice.

"Well, yes," Sophie said. "They're beautiful. You have so many."

"Years and years and years of treasure," Kolga sighed. "So much of it was here before I was even born. But Mother brings back more with every wreck. Sailors used to pad their pockets with gold, you know, back in the day. So that if the ship wrecked they would have gifts for Mother, and she might be pleased and spare them."

"Did she?" Sophie asked hesitantly, glancing over at Ran, who was dancing with Hefrig, spinning by their elbows, holding crab claws in their fists. She seemed the very source of happiness. Sophie couldn't imagine her wrecking a ship, drowning its passengers, stealing its bounty.

"Of course not," Kolga said snippily. "It doesn't work like that. You can't buy your way out of destiny. Mother does what the Dola tells her. But humans always think that *things* will save them." She said *things* with terrible scorn in her voice. "Take what you want," she said to Sophie, but it was not a warm offer. "We don't care about such stuff down here. We play with it, but it doesn't mean anything to us."

Sophie felt herself growing angry with this snobby maiden. "Easy for you to say," she snapped. "When you have so much. Things like this"—she looked around at the trunks of riches—"they *help* people on the earth. It—it buys them things."

"See?" Kolga said, raising an icy eyebrow. "Things to buy more things. Humans. Ridiculous."

"Some things are necessary," Sophie said, her voice rising. "People need *real* things, like food, or, or they need to pay rent, or pay to have lights in their house, so they can see, and they need to pay to see the doctor if they're sick, and a lot of people can't afford those things—"

"Well, it sounds awful," Kolga said. "Human life. Why don't you all do something about it if you hate it so much?"

"It's not that easy," Sophie said hotly. This maiden was impossible. "Do you even *know* any humans?"

"I walk amongst you from time to time," Kolga said in a bored voice. "But the things that interest you—it's like being amongst babies. I'd rather stay down here with my sisters."

"Well, we wouldn't like you, either!" Sophie said, and began piling chunky strands of gems around her neck. The stones were so heavy they cut into her collarbone. "And I guess I'll just help myself to these, then, if you're so above it all."

Kolga laughed, a string of frosty bubbles. She waved her blue-gray hand at Sophie, as if dismissing her.

"I'm walking away," Sophie said, "but I'm walking away because I don't want to talk to you. Not because you did *that*." Sophie swished her hand back at the maiden and stumbled away, her gait off balance with the heft of the jewels piled around her neck. She made her way to Syrena, who was speaking with Unnr in a low, happy voice.

"Sophie!" the mermaid welcomed. "We were just to speak of you!"

Unnr took note of Sophie's scowl and the hefty pile of jewels around her neck.

"Ah... were you just talking to Kolga?" the maiden asked.

"To talk to Kolga is to fight with Kolga!" Syrena said.

"She's terrible!" Sophie spat. "I don't understand how you all live down here, stealing treasures from people and drowning them, and then you act so happy to see me. Syrena, I want to leave!"

Unnr turned to Syrena and gave a sad little smile. "See?" she said. "It is very hard for us to be friendly with the humans, for this reason. They don't understand."

"But Sophie is Odmieńce," Syrena said. "A great race, like Jottnar. Sophie—" She smiled at the girl, placing a tender hand on Unnr's arm. "Jottnar much like Odmieńce. You practically cousins. Old, old people."

Ran drifted over to them and handed a lobster tail to Sophie. "Here, my love. Eat up."

"But you kill people," Sophie accused.

"Sophie!"

"How is this different than Kishka!" the girl demanded. "Kishka and her evils?"

"Kishka!" Ran gasped. "Oh, dear. Kishka—Kishka is of a different nature than the Jottnar. We are of the sea, we *are* the sea. We do the sea's bidding. The sea gives life and takes life, and we are its servants. In return, the sea gives us joy, and health, and family."

"And, like, a billion dollars worth of gold and diamonds," Sophie grumbled.

"Yes, true. They add much beauty. And I do adore beauty."

"She was talking to Kolga," Unnr said to her mother.

"Oh, my Kolga. I think humans would say she was born without a heart. But it is how she serves the sea. She makes its waters cold, and the shock of it helps the sailors go quicker. She is a mercy in her way. All my daughters help me."

"Me and Bara just sort of manage things," Unnr offered. "Bloo is mostly lazy, but she is helpful when the ships are battling. She only helps when there is war."

Sophie looked over at the maiden with the sticky red hair. She ate not from a platter of cooked fish but chomped into live ones, eating them slowly.

"Wars are hard," Ran said. "They are Kishka's work. But we cooperate with the sea, and we help to end it as swiftly as possible. Most of my daughters cannot bear the wars. To die by the sea, that is natural, destiny. To die by war, it is the work of evil. I am grateful that Bloo is so capable, to help with those calls."

"Dufa stirs the waters to confuse the sailors, spin them down." Unnr said. "This helps the boats sink. Hefrig is more of a clobberer. She's good if it is taking too long. She moves things along with a swift punch. And Hronn, she brings the sailors down. The last thing they know is Hronn's embrace."

"I have more daughters," Ran said proudly. "Bylgia works out in the deep, pushing the boats toward us. And Himinglaeva, she is the most beautiful. She floats along the vessels and brings pleasure at the sight of her. She brings the stars down to her belly and shimmers. She is delightful. I do wish you could meet all of my children. But—" She smiled at Syrena. "You are so close with my tenth daughter, the mermaid Syrena. I feel as if she is my own."

"After Griet," Syrena said, "after all that happen, I stay here for so long. I learn to cook food like Jottnar do, and make ale. I help with all the maidens, like, what you call—nanny? So many little maidens! Make me quite crazy. But so very nice to be among others. To know and see love, like I had for Griet. I thought my love was gone. It could have infected my heart and made me go bad. This is what Kishka hopes will happen. She hopes that we are weak-hearted, that we tip ourselves into hate. I could have gone about and brought pain to humans for what they did to Griet. And my wrath would double up inside my heart till it was huge and rotten inside me. Kishka would have sunk her teeth into me then, and I would not even know! But I come here—I see love. I learn my heart strong. Too strong for hatred." The mermaid laid her head on Unnr's arm.

"You do seem very good," Ran nodded, observing the mermaid. "Even better than last time, yes? You seem—happier."

"Is her." Syrena pointed a long, elegant finger at Sophie. "She do something. She try to take away all my pain, pain for Griet, and for other loss. Not good, but also, she do take away some bad things. We all have little bits of dirt on our hearts, ya? Sophie clean them up."

"And I will clean you up!"

Sophie ducked out of the way as Dufa came twisting toward Syrena, holding a great, lumpy sponge in her hands. "You are a mess! I never seen you look so scabby!"

Ran smiled and nodded as her daughter got busy loofahing the dried, torn scales from Syrena's tail. And to Sophie's surprise, Syrena seemed glad at the attention, smiling with pleasure as her scales started to shine.

Sophie noticed, as she bent to the mermaid, that Dufa's legs beneath her watery dress were also somewhat scaled, and her toes were webbed. Her hands too, clutching and working the sponge, had bits of shining web between the fingers. A look around at the others showed Sophie that all the Jottnar had these attributes—shining scales that climbed their legs beneath their clothing, and webbing that fanned their fingers and toes.

Sophie shivered as Kolga approached the two of them, holding a comb fashioned from fish bones. She began working the tangles from Syrena's hair. Unnr left to fetch a hollow piece of coral filled with something fatty she smeared across Syrena's tail, following the path of Dufa's sponge. Syrena sighed and—Sophie could not believe the sound—giggled.

"You maidens spoil me so," she said happily.

"And what of you?" Sophie turned to see Bloo, the most fearsome of the maidens, staring her down. "What is it you need?"

"Uh... nothing," Sophie said. "I'm good. I'm just a girl. I don't have, you know, tail problems or anything."

"Your hair is insulting," Bloo said. "I must fix it." And without asking permission, the maiden pulled a comb from her own crimson hair. She lifted the hem of her watery dress to wash away the sticky red from the tines. *Blood*, Sophie realized with a shiver. *That's blood in her hair.*

Bloo went to work sternly, pulling apart the great tangles that had snarled Sophie's hair. The girl protectively shielded the octopus. "Be careful," she said weakly.

"What is that octopus doing living on your head? We should eat him."

"No!" Sophie cried. "I like him. Please."

"And this?" Blooughadda held up the lock of Sophie's hair holding Livia's feather.

"Leave that!" Sophie snapped, tugging it away from the maiden. "That is my power."

Bloo smiled, her lips lifting up over her fanged teeth. "Well, well," she said. "Perhaps she is Odmieńce after all."

"Of course I'm Odmieńce," Sophie said haughtily. She was getting sick of these snotty maidens. "I turned myself into a shark and bit Kishka's head off!"

"Did you?" Bloo asked, her bloodshot eyes wide.

"She had tricked me into a giant shell, but I fought her, and I am here. I turned myself into a mermaid to escape the Swilkie. I can do many magics."

Bloo nodded, seeming somewhat humbled, and continued un-ratting the girl's hair. Sophie thought briefly of Andrea, how her mother had brushed her hair smooth at the start of this long voyage, before she said good-bye. But Bloo's nails were sharp and pricking. She got no comfort out of this maiden's touch. Sophie worried she had not savored that moment with her mother enough. She wished she had slowed time to make last her mother's sweet fingers sending goose bumps up her shoulders as she plaited her hair. That last demonstration of Andrea's complicated love. Sophie had no idea when she'd ever be touched by her mother again, or even see her.

Bloo let go of Sophie to fashion a crown from coral and fish bone, linking them together with a chain of gold and rubies. She wound Sophie's newly bouncy hair into a series of braids, pinning it here and there with fish bone. She laid the crown on her head, then placed the octopus inside.

"There," Bloo said. "You look much more beautiful now." She brought a reflective seashell up before Sophie's eyes, and Sophie barely recognized herself in it. Partly because it had been so long since she'd seen herself. Partly because she rarely looked so cleaned up and groomed. But also—she had grown. She was growing. She looked older than she remembered, less like a girl, more a woman. A young one, but still. There was the flash of something adult in her eye, something that shocked but delighted her.

"Thank you," she said to Bloo, who bent her head in return, and pinned her fish comb back in her mass of sticky red hair.

"I need something from you," Bloo said. "And you need it, too. I need you to look inside my heart."

"Why?" Sophie asked. She found she was not so afraid of Bloo, not as she had been even moments ago. Something about seeing herself in the seashell. *You forgot who you were,* Sophie thought. *You must not forget again. You are Odmieńce. Sophie Swankowski.* Even though Sophie still wasn't sure what this meant, she knew it meant something. And she would figure the rest out as she went along.

The Billow Maiden reached out and grabbed Sophie's hands in her own. Her nails were tipped with darkness, a darkness that went up and underneath the claw of her fingernails. Their tips dug into Sophie's skin just slightly, but she knew Bloo didn't mean to hurt her. It's just what her fingertips did.

"I know what I am, and what I do. I'm very good at it."

"Drowning sailors," Sophie said.

"Yes," Bloo nodded, oblivious to any judging tone in the girl's voice. "I work much less than my sisters. It is a strange sort of compromise— I see less death, but the death I do see is more terrible. But it is as if I were built for it. I swim out to the ships, and the redder the water, the more alive I feel. It's as if there is an animal where my heart should be, and it comes alive then, and I know what to do."

The earnestness in Bloo's face, almost a tenderness, melted Sophie's bad feelings toward her. "You're like a shark," she said aloud, more for her own understanding than for Bloo.

"Yes. There are many creatures down here that do killing. Most of us, in fact. I am more akin to a shark than, say, an octopus," the maiden said, reaching out and petting the octopus on Sophie's head. "But, Sophie"—Bloo's hands came back and clutched at Sophie's painfully—"I must know that there is no evil in my heart for this. I can… enjoy my work. I know it sounds strange to you. My parents, my sister, the Dola, all insist it is my nature, and as such is not evil. But I have finally met someone who can look into my heart and say for certain." Her grip intensified, and a nail brought a small prick of blood from Sophie's hand.

"Okay—but why did you say I need this, too?" Sophie pulled her hands away, sucking on her tiny wound.

"I see this is getting to you," Bloo said softly. "My family. What we do. And Syrena, her pain, I heard her speaking about how you tried to take it. It sounds like you need to understand what is the good badness and what is the bad badness."

There was a pause while Sophie considered Bloo's words, and then she burst out, "This is making me crazy!" Then she just couldn't stop. "I didn't realize this would be so hard! Leaving my family, I knew that would be hard, and I knew it would be hard to travel with Syrena because she can be sort of mean, and I can hardly wrap my head around whatever I need to do to Kishka, who is still, in spite of everything, my grandmother, you know? I know that is going to be *really* tough, like,

I know I'm going to need therapy after all this. But you want me to figure out the *bad* badness from the good badness? That sounds impossible."

In the roar of the revelry around them Sophie's outburst was unheard by anyone but Bloo. The maiden took Sophie by her hand, and the fight went out of the girl. She allowed the maiden to lead her down a gilded hallway and into a chamber hung with tapestries and tossed with fat velvet pillows. Sophie followed Bloo's lead and sat down on one of them. The tapestry facing her depicted a lone unicorn with a long, slender horn. Behind it were droopy willow trees and a pale blue sky.

"Are these guys for real, too?" Sophie asked, gesturing to the artwork.

"Unicorns?" Bloo asked. "Oh, yes, of course. I mean, they were. They haven't done well with the changes on earth. Very sensitive creatures. I think there are some left, but they don't grow horns anymore, and they have quite lost their magic. But they were so beautiful, weren't they? In their day." Bloo shifted into a comfortable position and looked at Sophie expectantly. "So, what should I do?"

"Oh—um, nothing," Sophie shrugged. "Just be comfortable, I suppose. I do it."

"Are you ready?"

"I guess so."

"Then do it already." Bloo swatted at Sophie like a cat, leaving tiny red scratches.

"Ow!"

"Oh, sorry. Sorry. Just—you know, let's go. Before someone comes for us. My family *hates* when anyone goes off by themselves. It's all 'Come be happy, come be happy' all the time."

Sophie snorted. "That's kind of great," she said. "I wish my mom was as happy as your mom."

"It's harder for humans," Bloo said. "It's so stressful. Your lives are so short you don't really have time to figure out how to get it together. But please—me. Can you look at my heart, please?"

SO SOPHIE DID. With the slightest push she was inside Blooughadda. It was a vast place, much bigger than the maiden herself. Not the tight, sick interior of Laurie LeClair, or the tough terrain of Angel. Not her mother's claustrophobic, anxious heart or Livia's—Livia!—compact pigeon heart full of love. Bloo's heart was a windy place, wide enough to have weather. It was like its own land. Sophie couldn't tell if she saw craggy rocks, tough green shoots fighting through the cracks, or if that was just what Bloo's heart felt like. Like something that had been there forever. Like the heart of the earth itself.

Sophie pushed in deeper, feeling no resistance from the Billow Maiden. The atmosphere grew humid, and Sophie knew she was getting to the real stuff, whatever it was. The stuff that mattered. She didn't feel afraid, because Bloo's heart was deep and good. There was love in here, old and abiding. For her family and for the ocean. As she pushed through it, the love entered Sophie as well, contagious, as love should be. She felt a great swell of affection for the Jottnar, their jolliness, their extreme good nature. But still, Sophie moved forward, seeking. The mist grew hotter, and Sophie could feel it in her lungs. Like when she was little and had a bad cough, the croup, and her mother had sat her in the bathroom with the shower on full blast, creating clouds of steam that filled the room and curled around her.

Sophie went deeper, looking for the source of that heat. The landscape was gone. It was only crimson and darkness here, something glowing embedded in the rock wall of a cave. Sophie could feel it; it practically pulsed. Sophie approached it like coming up on a sleeping beast. This was the heart of Blooughadda's heart. As if the heart had a heart of its own, and Bloo's was like a sleeping dog, ready to snap at whatever disturbed its dreams. Sophie could imagine what woke it up. Blood, war, the smell of men sweating out the toxins of hatred in battle.

Sophie sat beside Bloo's heart of hearts. She imagined herself upon a pillow, much as her body was back in the chamber. She sat calmly and breathed. With her mind and her own heart, she touched it. She could feel memories in the air around it—oh, how sharply she felt them! She was moving slowly, but the punch of memories was unexpected. The piercing eye of a sailor, close to death, thrashing. Sophie breathed it in, the sailor's final terror, Bloo's fleeting feeling of grief. A great stain of red blotted her vision, as if the maiden had wrapped her hair around her face. It was the blood of war, and she felt in Bloo's heart something dull and constant. It felt like *No*. Bloo's refusal that this was the way. That this had to be. Sophie stepped back from the *No*, though she could feel the hurt it brought the maiden. There was love in this hurt. It stayed.

She moved toward something that spun thick and gray, a cobweb. Every thread of it tangled into the other, and it was sticky. It clung to Sophie and she experienced the maiden's confusion, her guilt at her very nature. Sophie took it. She breathed it in.

This glowing thing in the rock wall, bright as molten lava, it had a sheen now, like hot glass. It glistened. Sophie pushed into it gingerly, like dipping her toe in an ocean. The feeling, hot and strong, knocked her down. Like a fireball had shot through her—not exactly electric, but like the breath of god, or a gate of hell swung open. Sophie lay where she landed, down but not out, and breathed herself calm again. What was that? An alarm, a warning system.

Bloo's heart of hearts was protecting her from what it contained—instinct, blood lust. It was a wolf; it wanted what it wanted. It was animal, it was nature. And it was fed by that other thing, the *No.* The grief at war worked to temper Bloo's native impulse, and together they shielded the rest of the maiden's heart from its hungry wildness.

Sophie moved backward, away from the scorching glow, back through the mist of love until that too cooled and dried and she was back by the crags, their tough landscape of ancient rock and persistent life that sprung from it. Sophie came back.

Chapter 18

Inside Bloo's chamber Sophie was splayed on her back, and it felt like one of the boulders she'd imagined was crushing her chest. She saw the unicorn, noble and stoic in the tapestry above her, and then Bloo, gripping her, her claws tearing holes in Sophie's linen garment.

"Sophie!" the maiden hissed. "Sophie! Are you okay? What do you need?"

"Salt," Sophie creaked, finding her throat so dry—parched—that it seemed to cling to itself. She could barely speak.

"All around you," Bloo gestured. "We are in the ocean."

"More," Sophie managed. Then, "Please."

Bloo vanished in a cloud of pink water, and was back swiftly, the Dola in tow.

"Help her," Bloo demanded.

"Yesssss," Sophie squeaked at the sight of the Ogresses' salt, worn as a bead around the dolphin's neck. It was smaller than it had been at the start of their journey, but there was enough. "That," she lifted her hand weakly, pointing at the rock. Bloo used her fingernails to slice the rope that knotted it to the dolphin's body and handed the salt to Sophie, who began to gnaw.

Oh, salt! It zinged her like a wonderful shock, like a battery charged. It quenched a thirst deeper than water, brought wetness back to her body. She broke off a piece with her back molars and sucked it, let the juice of it fall back down her throat. She crunched a great mouthful, straining it through her teeth.

Bloo laughed at the sight of her, clapping her hands joyfully. "You are happy!" she cried. "I have not seen you happy since you arrived at Laeso Island! Had anyone known all it took was some salt, well, we would have brought you bricks of it!"

"It helps me," Sophie said simply, noting that Bloo, too, seemed happier than she had been. "When I do that stuff."

"What did you do to me?" The maiden ruffled her robes, touching herself, as if what had happened could be felt upon her body.

"I did what you asked," Sophie said. "I looked in on your heart."

"And?"

"Jottnar have such complicated hearts!" Sophie marveled. "So much more complicated than humans."

"Well, that would make sense," Bloo nodded. "All things considered." She looked proud.

"It's like, you have a heart inside your heart. And the heart that does the, the—"

"The killing, yes."

"It sort of protects the rest of the heart from it. And you're sad about it all. And some sadness I took away—"

"I can feel it!" the Billow Maiden cried.

"—but most of it had to stay."

"Of course," Bloo nodded solemnly.

"Your sadness is so important," Sophie mused. "It's actually stopping your heart of hearts from feeding on hate. Your heart of hearts—it's very scary, it's sort of like a monster."

"Yes," Bloo nodded. "It feels like a monster."

"But it's not a bad monster. It wants it all to stop—the war, the blood."

"I can't make it stop," Bloo whispered.

"No," Sophie affirmed. "You can't."

Bloo was silent for a moment, and then she took Sophie's hand again. "But you can," she said. "And that's why you're here."

BACK IN THE great hall, Ran and her daughters were whooping and ululating, making strange, wild cries flow from their throats. Aegir stood behind them, stirring a large cauldron of ale, watching silently. His eyes above his great beard seemed full of pride and awe.

"What's going on?" Sophie asked Bloo. She had become accustomed to the little stabs of the maiden's fingernails. It was worth it, she'd decided, to have such friendship with the creature.

"It's time to go," Bloo said, her eyes on her family. "They've been summoned."

"You're not needed," said the Dola to Blooughadda. "It's not a battle."

"Well, that is sweet news," Bloo nodded.

"What is it?" Sophie asked. "Are they going to—are they—sinking?"

"There is a submarine," the Dola said simply. "A research vessel. It is headed to the waters near the Ogresses' cave, into the depths."

"And I guess it won't make it," Sophie said, a chilly dread coursing down her spine.

"It is not meant to," said the Dola. "But it is not an accident that you are here, Sophia. You are meant to be. You are meant to join the Jottnar. There is something for you to see."

Sophie looked anxiously at Bloo, as if for help, but Bloo just looked at the Dola.

"But—I would rather not. I don't think I'm ready to see something so awful."

"You must," the Dola stated. "Gather yourself."

Sophie had no clue as to how to prepare to sink a submarine with a bunch of nonhuman ocean goddesses. Angel and the pigeons had maybe forgotten to prep her for this one. Syrena, too. Sophie scanned the great hall for the mermaid, but she didn't see her.

"Where is Syrena?" she asked the Dola, a tad desperately. "She'll come, too, right?"

"No," said the Dola. "There is no need for her to be there. Syrena is resting."

"Bloo?" Sophie squeezed the maiden's hand so hard that her own chewed-up fingernails cut into her skin. The maiden shook her head.

"I only go when I must, and that is bad enough. I will stay behind with Syrena. But if the Dola says you must go, then of course you must. There is no argument."

Sophie nodded. She had engaged in arguments with the Dola before.

And with that, the water around Sophie became filled with currents and fluctuating temperatures as the Billow Maidens, led by Ran, rushed toward her.

"Come!" Hefrig shouted to Sophie, reaching out and yanking her into the throng of them with a short but powerful wave.

"Bloo!" Sophie hollered, and the maiden waved her on.

"I will see you when you return."

And with that Sophie was caught up in the advancing waves of the Jottnar. They propelled themselves out into the sea, down, down, down. Dufa swam up above them, creating small dust devils of water as she went. As the ocean darkened and they left behind the honeyeyed glow of the Jottnar cave, Sophie lost sight of her. They traveled far and fast.

They came upon a deep place jagged with rock and the bones of ships that the Jottnar must have wrecked long ago. There was already something creepy about the place—like it was meant to be a place of death alone. Insectlike creatures skittered here and there, dining on dead things, looking to Sophie like giant underwater cockroaches. She shuddered. Schools of cod circled like ghosts, their eyes spooky, empty.

Spiny urchins clustered at the base of the shipwreck like a tiny, menacing army. Seaweed slapped heavily in the currents.

And then the submarine appeared. It came down in the wake of Dufa's spinning, an underwater tornado, the vessel caught in the midst of it being flung this way and that, all of its alarm lights flashing in the deep—red and white and blue. Sophie's heart tightened, her throat too, so that she felt like she couldn't breathe. She swam away as it crashed down into the rocks, trying hard to swallow, to take a slow, shallow breath. Sophie could hear the alarm systems, shrill and urgent. There were humans inside that submarine. And they were going to die here.

Kolga swam in circles around the impact zone, chilling the waters. Unnr and Bara rocked the submarine with waves punctuated by Hefrig's stronger punches, knocking the people inside the vessel off their feet as they tried to understand what was happening.

The Billow Maidens moved so swiftly in the water that the men inside the submarine could not see them. They were in their element, they were the element. They were the ocean, spinning and lapping and pounding.

But Sophie. Had she thought to, she could have hollered a zawolanie and become anything at all. But she was frozen with horror by the scene—an Odmieńce, but also a girl. A human girl. And through their windows the scientists in the submarine could see her.

Behind the curving glass of the submarine's window, a man stared into Sophie's eyes, his mouth hanging open in shock. Sophie took a quick inventory of her appearance—her neat braids and shining crown and strange outfit of linen and leather and weeds, a pile of jewels around her neck. She must look like a kid playing dress-up in a toy treasure chest. From inside herself Sophie moved close to the man, close enough to hear his thoughts: *This is the beginning, I am hallucinating, losing oxygen, already dreaming.* And as if the thoughts were an invitation, Sophie hurled herself into him.

The fear, the stark terror of death was a roar, a reflex, the strain of every cell in the man's body deciding to fight or flee. His mind was sharp and orderly as a computer, working to make sense of what was happening, and she understood that he was a scientist, that this was the way he thought of the world—*submarine suddenly sucked down, a vortex of sorts, had heard of such things, the girl, the girl, there seems to be oxygen, I'm still breathing.* And his heart, plummeting faster than his vessel as it ran through every earthly thing he loved, people, places, things. Sophie saw flashes of smiling faces and a cozy cabin roofed with seaweed that looked out onto calm waters, she saw a dog, she saw the man's happy life above the waves. And as Hefrig delivered the blow that shattered the glass, as Hronn rushed toward the man and wrapped herself around him, Sophie reached deep into his heart and removed all the fear, all the pain, so that the love the man had for his life surged through him. She felt his head go light and he began to cry for how beautiful it had been, his existence, and how grateful he was for it. How he had loved his work. Sophie could hear pieces of it, words and phrases she did not understand, but some that resonated, *dark matter, dark energy, universe, expansion*—and, as she looked into his eyes, *the computer, the computer, the computer, please take the computer.*

All this transpired in a few seconds, but it was the long, long moment of the dying, the slowed-down time at the bottom of the ocean. Then the man was gone, and Ran was laying him gently in a patch of sand. Sophie looked down at him, dazed, heartbroken. Tears spilled from her eyes and merged into the great sea that surrounded them all. Ran looked up at her.

"I never—" Sophie sputtered. "I've never seen a person die before." She heaved with sobs, trying to catch her breath. She couldn't get the taste of his fear out of her mouth. To have seen his death, to have been witness, would have been awful enough. But to have been inside his heart at his last moment—Sophie shuddered, felt her own heart heavy inside her like a hunk of lead.

"No time for mourning, Sophie," Ran said, gentle but firm. "There are others. And you can help them. You must."

Sophie turned back to the submarine and saw the other scientists struggling against the water. Without hesitating, she leapt into them, quelling their fear and illuminating the love in their hearts, giving them peace. She worked with the Jottnar, and as each scientist passed she heard some of the same words in their minds that she had heard in the first man—*dark energy, source, universe, dark matter, the computer, the computer.*

Chapter 19

When they were done, the Billow Maidens slowed their work until they appeared again not as the ocean itself but as women, and they looked upon Sophie with widened eyes.

"My dear," Ran began, draping her elegant arm around Sophie. "That was positively magnificent. That was the most elegant, peaceful, truly lovely death we have ever delivered." Her daughters nodded furiously, their eyes stuck on Sophie, wordless. Sophie could not be sure in the hazy deep, but she thought she saw an icy blue tear slide down Kolga's blue-gray cheek.

Hronn rushed to her and strangled the girl in a suffocating embrace. "Oh, could you teach me how to do that?" she begged. "My work would be so improved! What is our magic?"

"No, it is for Sophia only," Ran told her daughter. "It is her magic alone. The magic of half-Odmieńce, half-human girl."

Sophie startled a bit at that. "It's Odmieńce," she said to Ran. "My magic. Humans aren't magic."

Ran smiled. "Everything has its magic. Humans can't see their own. But your ability, this—thing you do. It is so particular. It is the powers of the Odmieńce, of course, but it those powers mixed with the magic of the human heart. It is a particularly human magic, Sophia. Which is good, because it is the humans you are meant to help."

Sophie looked down at the scientists in the wet sand around them. Hronn had closed their eyes with kisses as she took them down. They looked peaceful sleeping, but the dread Sophie had lifted from them had gathered into her heart and stuck there, throbbing. Her tears swirled in the water before her face.

"I don't feel like I helped," she said.

"Oh, but you did!" Kolga shouted. "Even I could feel it." The maiden touched the spot on her chest where the feeling had occurred, the place where hearts beat inside the creatures that have them.

"It is why the Dola brought you," Dufa hiccupped.

"I guess so," Sophie said, uncertain. She was glad that she had been there to make their last moments more peaceful, but what was so special about these humans that the Dola would want Sophie to help them? Weren't there people dying everywhere, all the time? Why was it her destiny to be here?

Sophie swam toward the crashed submarine and squeezed inside through a smashed-out window. It was still lit up; soon the lights would dim, but for a while they would remain bright, flashing, the ship sounding its useless alarm to no one.

Sophie was surprised at how large the thing was. There were many rooms, and so many instruments and machines. Sophie realized what it must take to keep such a thing running so far down here, and she thought about where it had been headed with all these scientists aboard, into the deep, deep sea where the Ogresses lived. Sophie remembered when she had stood before the Invisible in the waters outside the cavern, how Syrena had told her about the scientists that had dropped equipment there to study it. What had they been hoping to find?

In one of the submarine's chambers, what seemed to be an office, Sophie came upon a package. It was bundled in a thick, waterproof plastic casing, and through it Sophie could make out a laptop. She lifted it and noted its weight, feeling the shifting thump of papers inside. The dying thoughts of the scientist were still haunting her heart. *The computer, the computer, the computer.* There were probably lots of computers in the submarine; really, the machine itself was like one huge computer. Sophie wished the man still lived, so she could enter his heart and ask him, *This one?* She didn't want to let him down. But Sophie was the only creature breathing inside the crashed submarine. Any other computer in the submarine was already waterlogged. She swam back out of the vessel, the package gathered in her arms.

Ran and the Billow Maidens were arranged outside the submarine, waiting for her. Ran nodded when she saw what Sophie held in her arms.

"Bounty," she said. "It is fair to take it. No insult to anything or anyone."

"It's not that," Sophie shook her head. "It's not a treasure or anything. It's a computer. And some papers, I think."

"Then why do you want it?" asked Kolga.

"I think I'm meant to have it," Sophie said. "Maybe it will explain what they were doing. Why I'm here. The scientist—when he died, he was thinking about it."

Ran nodded. "Well, the Dola will let you know if you're wrong."

"That's for sure," snorted Hronn.

Sophie didn't need to harness the water, she simply rode upon the Billow Maidens as one would body surf a current, hugging the plastic package to her chest. She felt her spirits lift when the amber glow of Laeso Island came into view, faint at first and quickly becoming a glowing path that drew them in. Sophie understood now why Syrena held this place so close to her heart. It was truly a special place, and the Jottnar a special people.

IN THE GREAT hall Aegir had fixed a mighty stew and Sophie found herself as hungry as a Billow Maiden, devouring deep seashells full of the salty, umami goodness. She heard Ran bragging about her as she slurped and slurped.

"It was incredible. Like nothing we've seen. Just—this peace. A peace and a love for life. She brought it to them."

"No," Sophie corrected, swallowing a scallop. "They had it inside them. I just... brought it out. I took away everything that was covering it up."

"But how do you feel, Sophie?" Syrena swam up to her, touched her shoulders and looked deeply into her eyes. "I know it must have been shock to you, to see that. Have you recovered?"

"I'm fine," Sophie shrugged. Deep in her heart she knew the answer was more complicated, but it was also for her alone, the one human in the room. "I don't need salt. Though this"—she shook her shell at the chef, hoping to change the subject—"is the best, saltiest stew I've ever had." Aegir smiled and held his own shell out to her in a toast.

"She bounced right back," Ran said proudly. "I saw her."

"And what is this?" Syrena seemed to sense that Sophie didn't want to dwell on the topic, and she touched the package in Sophie's arms.

"A computer," Sophie said. "I took it from the submarine. They wanted me to."

"Whatever for?" the mermaid asked, taking it from her arms. She began to tug at the plastic. "You need to check your—how is it?—Facebook from underwater? You want to Tweet Laeso Island?"

"Don't!" Sophie grabbed it back. "It's waterproofed. I can't open it down here. It will have to wait till Poland."

"It's heavy!" Syrena said. "You think to carry all the way to Vistula River? To swim with it?"

Sophie shrugged. "I guess so. I don't know how else to open it. I can't open it down here, right?"

"No, not a computer," Bloo nodded. "Or paper. It will disintegrate."

"Well, I not carrying it all the way home," Syrena said. "So don't ask me."

"I didn't!" Sophie said. "I'll take care of it."

"Why do you want?"

"I don't know," Sophie admitted. "I think it will tell us what the scientists were doing down here. It was—I heard their thoughts. I think it's important. The submarine was on its way to the Ogresses'. To the Invisible, maybe."

"Scientists don't understand the Invisible," Syrena scoffed. "That why they going there."

"Well, whatever they know, I want to know," Sophie insisted. "I heard their thoughts as they were dying. They were thinking of the universe, and of darkness and energy."

"You make plan based on last thoughts of dying person?" Syrena asked. "Maybe not person's best moment."

"I could tell what was fear, I took it away. This was something else."

"She did," Ran said, coming up behind the girl and placing her large, elegant hands upon her shoulders. "We all could see it. We could *feel* it."

"The Dola said I was meant to be there. To see something. Is the Dola still here?"

"No." Bloo shook her head. "The dolphin is still here, but it's just a dolphin now."

Sophie gazed out at the pod, playing as they waited for Sophie and Syrena. She spotted the one the Dola had inhabited. It was back with its fellows, leaping and nosing around. Sophie felt a tug of longing. She wished she'd gotten to say good-bye to the stupid Dola. She wished she could have shown the Dola her package and asked, *This? Is this what I am meant to have?* But the simple fact that the Dola wasn't there perhaps confirmed it. It was her destiny.

"Well, we learn everything in Poland," Syrena nodded. "But your arms be sore, carrying that so far!"

"In Poland I come out of the water, right?"

"Right," Syrena nodded. Sophie brightened at the thought. Sunshine, fresh air, regular movement. Syrena looked skeptical. "Do not be so happy. Will be hard. Should know that."

"Okay," Sophie said. "But then I get sunshine back, right?"

"Ya. You get your sun. I do, too. I river mermaid now. Much used to sunshine myself."

AS SYRENA AND Sophie prepared to leave Laeso Island, Kolga swooshed up to Sophie in her current of chilly water.

"Sorry about that," the maiden said sheepishly to Sophie, watching her shiver. "I can't help it."

"It's quite all right," Sophie said. Kolga reached out and touched her, running her hand up and down Sophie's arms, rolling with goose bumps.

"So interesting," Kolga said. "I myself don't really feel the cold. I just *am* it."

She held out a backpack. It was roomy, canvas, army-issue. The buttons had started to rust, but Sophie could make out the mark of an anchor stamped upon the metal. There were handsome striped patches decorating it. She offered the pack to Sophie.

"I thought you could put your thing in this, while you travel. I think the straps go over your shoulders—"

"Yes, it's a backpack," Sophie said. "I have one at home." Of course, the one back at home was small, fit for her own body, not a man's. Sophie tugged the straps tight, but the bag still sagged down her back. Still, she supposed it was better than nothing. And she liked the rugged look of it. She slid her package inside and, after a thought, removed the heap of gold and jewels she'd rebelliously looped around her neck. There were so many strands she could not hold them all in her hands, and some slid loose, falling into the sand like bejeweled eels.

"I'm sorry I was so rude," she apologized to Kolga. Sophie didn't need to go inside the Billow Maiden to understand that Kolga's coldness was no more personal than the coldness of snow, the sharpness of icicles. She might not have a heart as Sophie had come to understand such a thing, but she had what she needed, and the same forces that had created everything else had created her.

Kolga bent and snatched up the fallen jewels, slid them into Sophie's backpack. "You can have all of them. I want you to, please. Enjoy them. Trade them for food, whatever you need them for. I am lacking in certain intelligence," she confessed without shame. "I have a very strong mind, strong instincts. But without a heart there are many things I can't comprehend. Human things, especially."

Sophie dropped the mound of necklaces into her backpack. It weighed her down, but she couldn't resist the treasure. She wanted to show the jewels to Ella, to give her some, to give some to Andrea, to Angel. Angel wouldn't wear such things, Sophie imagined, but she could sell them and have more money for her and her mother.

"What about the crown?" Kolga asked. "Should I help you with it?"

Sophie's hand rose up to her head, where she felt the chalky toughness of the coral and the ridges of the seashells, the smooth chunks of gems and the heavy golden links. She gave the little octopus a pat and was startled to feel how it had grown. *It's a baby,* she thought. *Not a teacup octopus. Not a miniature. It will grow.*

"No," she told Kolga. "I think I'd like to wear it."

"It suits you," the maiden nodded. "You look more regal than when you arrived, more..." She searched for the words, then gave up. "You look more the way I expected you to look. Having heard so much about you for so long."

Chapter 20

It took forever for Syrena to extricate herself from the endless round of hugs the Jottnar heaped upon her. Sophie watched as the mermaid lifted Hronn's hands off her, holding them in the air.

"Take her!" she cried. "Someone take her, or I will never get home to my river!"

Ran stepped up and grabbed her daughter, redirecting her embrace. Hronn hung on her mother so that their two robes flowed together as one. "Travel safe to your home," she said, "and please remember that this is your home as well. You too, Sophie." She smiled at the girl. "You are always welcome at Laeso Island."

"Thank you, "Sophie said. "I really hope to see you all again."

"You will," Bloo said with a smile. "The Dola told us."

Ran stared in amazement at Blooughadda's face. "A smile," she said. "I haven't seen this one smile since she was a wavelette. Your magic is evident, dear Sophie!"

"It was my pleasure," Sophie said humbly, almost shyly. She had entered the Jottnar home so confused by them, so overwhelmed and condemning. She was happy her departure was different. They were in her heart now, even cold Kolga, even and especially bloodthirsty Blooughadda. "It was an honor," she addressed the maiden, "to visit your complicated heart."

"It was an honor to host you," Bloo replied, bowing her head. They were like two queens regarding one another. With her crown on her brow and her backpack heavy on her back, Sophie commanded the waters and, alongside Syrena, she left Laeso Island, a chorus of love at their backs.

IT WAS THE Dola who had evicted the mermaid from her home on Laeso Island, back when she was a young mermaid who had just lost her sister. In the form of a seal, the Dola had glided into the golden chambers where Syrena was tending the Billow Maidens. The maidens all trilled with glee at the sight of the slick, whiskered animal, but Syrena rose quickly and put herself before them, considering the creature, then the girls. They were no longer babies, or toddlers either. They were big enough to fend off a hungry seal, and there were many of them, nine in total. Plus there was Syrena, her narwhal tusk never far from her grasp. And just one seal, plump, well fed. The mermaid relaxed.

"May they pet you?" she asked the seal, holding back the tide of maidens who swirled around her legs, in love with the sweet-faced creature. And the seal answered not in the seal squeals she'd learned to understand, but in the language of mermaids—though spoken in the chilling voice of the soulless.

"They may pet the seal, but it is you I have come for, Syrena."

The mermaid's tail went numb and her heart grew sore at the sound of the being's voice. The Billow Maidens backed away, and the more sensitive among them began to cry. "Shush," Syrena scolded them, fighting back her own sob. "Go to your *Moder*. Go now—tell her the Dola has come." The myth Syrena had been raised with was that one would always know the Dola if the creature came for you, and now she found the myth was true. Syrena's spine was cold, as if formed from vertebrae of ice. The maidens scuttled back into the cave.

"What is it?" Syrena said to the Dola. "You have already taken my sister and destroyed my village. You have made us barren creatures and sent us scattered through the seas. What more do you want to take from me? Go on. Take it." The being's coldness had infected her heart, and the mermaid supposed it was for the best. She wanted to face her destiny with dignity, and if the coldness of her heart could freeze her tears of hurt and fear before they slid down her cheeks, then all the better.

"You are mistaken," the Dola said. "You are confusing me for your destiny, and I am not. Your destiny is quite separate from me. I am but its messenger."

"Never mind," Syrena said coolly. "You are here to tell me I am to die, or to hurt someone I love. I've heard your legend my whole life. I'm to eat those babies I just was caring for, or I'm to fling myself into a shiver of sharks. Well, go on then. Deliver your message."

The seal's whiskers twitched on its soft black nose. Syrena bristled at the insult of it, that she would have such terrible news delivered from the snout of this adorable creature. There was no end to life's humiliations, the mermaid thought morosely.

"My more spectacular jobs tend to precede me," the Dola said, shrugging its slender seal shoulders. "No one ever talks about the time I make someone eat a meal they thought they were too full to eat. To take a different path to the green grocer. Such minutia makes the bulk of my work, you know, and it would bore you to tears. A thrill-seeking mermaid like you couldn't bear the reality of my job. And what about the nice things I do? When I rescue a lover from the grip of war and return them unscathed to their beloved, who has been *faithful*. No one discusses those jobs. Only the ones where the gladiator succumbs to the hippo. Where the midwife arrives sick from drink to deliver the child."

"So what will it be?" Syrena snapped. "Am I to be speared by pirates and have my tail nailed to the side of their ship? Or am I to fall in love with a giant squid? Make it snappy, please."

"You are to leave Laeso Island," the Dola said, and with that the seal spun and headed out the way it came.

"What?" Syrena dashed after the creature, snagging its stubby tail in the hands. "I need more than that! What else? What for?"

The Dola gazed at the mermaid, its stare hitting her like an icicle in the heart. "You have overstayed your time here, and I think you are aware of this. You took refuge, but now you hide. You must return to the waters."

"I was going to!" Syrena snapped, insulted. "I'm not *hiding*. I'm caring for the Billow Maidens. I'm helping Ran. I fully intend to return to the waters."

"You will return now. Your time here is ended. You know this to be true."

"I will leave as I please."

"I will inhabit the babies," the Dola said simply. "I will hop inside them and drive you mad. First Ran will be driven mad, and she will be overtaken by anger at you for not obeying, for leaving her daughters vulnerable to me. Then you will go mad, from the love you found here being ruined by your own stubbornness."

The dread in Syrena's heart swelled. Legend had it that the Dola only inhabited the form of a child in very dire circumstances, and to witness such coldness through the mouth of the babe could drive a being permanently mad. "Fine," Syrena said. "I will do what I must do." The mermaid bowed her head in a slight gesture of contrition.

The seal bobbed before her. "I know," the Dola said simply, and then was gone. And then Syrena was looking into the gentle brown eyes of a seal, nothing more. She called for the children to come and play with it.

SYRENA STEELED HERSELF for the next phase of her journey. She steeled herself for loneliness, for traveling without a companion, without her beloved Griet, away from the cacophonous joy of the Jottnar. She braced herself for battle. She would encounter sharks and other animals that would take advantage of her solitude—human animals foremost among them. She clasped her horn. Back at Laeso Island the tusk had not been needed, had become another curiosity in an underwater palace decorated with them. But once in the Kattegat it was a weapon, a mighty one. It consoled Syrena greatly. *You have the narwhal horn,* she reminded herself as the channels got thinner, the boats closer. *You are fearsome, a warrior. No threat will come to you.*

And for many miles, none did. The seas were teeming with life, and she feasted heartily. She had never been so close to the land, and began to enjoy navigating the bundles of rocks and small islands that clumped the waterways. Sometimes, when the moon was at its darkest, she would pull herself upon a crag and feel the air upon her, gaze up at the stars that sprinkled the sky. She would feel so small then, and it was a sweet, sad comfort. She was but a creature in the sea, no more, no less. She would find her way. Perhaps she was finding it a bit more each day.

Little did Syrena know, she was indeed spotted by humans during this winding part of her journey. But she was so close to where her sister had perished that the villagers there knew her story, and not even the gruffest among them wished to bother her. Some were scared, as the legend of her threat of war still loomed as a possibility. Others felt their hearts grow full with shame at their own kind, that any among them would hurt such a creature. The villagers hung back from the shore, giving the mermaid her space and making sure that she would enjoy safe passage. And so it was through her own cunning maneuvers and the kindness of humans that Syrena passed easily through the Kattegat, overcome with relief as her world opened up into the great Baltic Sea.

Chapter 21

"**I** have not traveled this route since I was such young mermaid," Syrena said as she and Sophie swam south from the Jottnar. Her deep sigh blew bubbles of air from the gills behind her ears, making her look, for one brief moment, as if she were wearing a magnificent silver headdress. "I am much glad to see Ran and her daughters before we come here. Their love make me strong. This is sad place for me."

"Is this—this is—"

"This where Griet lay, yes. Where she taken from me, where she die. Where she pushed out to the sea. Griet is all through the waters but here, here she is most strong. So I must be most strong too, ya?" Syrena looked at her charge and smiled at the girl. "You help make me strong, Sophia. You clean my heart, and you be here with me, you give me someone more to love. And love makes heart strong."

From atop her platform of ocean, Sophie could hardly believe her ears. Did Syrena just say she *loved* her? A rush of emotion—excitement

or anxiety, she couldn't tell—swept the girl's heart and she was speech-less. Had she felt any such love back at the Ogresses', when she pried inside the mermaid? She could not remember—all she dug at was the grief, the sorrow, feelings so mammoth they knocked her out. Without hesitation, Sophie plunged into the mermaid. She wasn't looking for sadness now, but love—and love she found. Syrena's interior was awash with it, completely flooded. A sea inside a sea maiden, it twinkled with salt and held currents of tragedy, tidal pulls of fearsome moods, but all of it within the liquid body of love. And Sophie found herself there, the tenderness the mermaid felt for her, the lessons she'd learned tug-ging her willful charge from the new world to the old. What was the flavor of this love? Pride, it was flavored with pride. Syrena was proud of her, and proud of herself, for the highs and lows of their unfinished journey. *Their* journey. Syrena's love for her was tied to her love for herself, much the way her love for Griet had existed during their time together. She and Syrena were a team, a pair. They were partners now, sisters. And Sophie realized she did not need to push and pull against the mermaid for her respect and concern. The mermaid held her in highest regard.

She pulled away as they sailed through the water. "I didn't know," Sophie said.

"Well, has been complicated." Syrena shrugged. "Love a living thing. Grows and changes. But we have arrived in this place, ya? We have arrived together, and we are good."

"Yes," Sophie nodded. She didn't want to ruin the moment by, like, bursting into tears or gushing, *I love you, too!* The mermaid's love was a noble love, and Sophie wanted to be worthy of it. "Yes," the girl agreed. "We have arrived together."

AS THEY MOVED toward the Baltic Sea, the water around them grew an icy shade of blue, and in the distance Sophie could see pods of beluga whales, white as ghosts, swirling together, creating whirls and currents. A school of cod came upon them, making their world momentarily silver, and Sophie, suddenly hungry, reached out her hand and snagged one. Like any other animal of the sea, she bared her teeth and ate.

She awaited the rest of the mermaid's story. It seemed to Sophie then the most precious gift anyone could give another, their story. In a world where everything can be stripped away by the whims of fortune, it was all that remained, stuck inside your body like an organ. To offer someone your story was like offering them your heart, Sophie realized, and she wondered if she was beginning to think like a poet, and if Syrena would be pleased. She watched the mermaid regard the sea around them with recognition and wonder, reaching out her hands so that the waters streamed through her elegant fingers, twirling through her rings of shell and coral. It was as if Syrena was reading the sea, as if she could feel the difference between these waters and all the waters in their wake.

As she watched the mermaid, Sophie had a chilling feeling of someone watching her, watching them both as they made their way out from the Kattegat and into the sea that would bring them, finally, to Poland. She knew it was her grandmother, and that the eye had been upon her all the while.

I know you see me, Sophie thought fiercely inside her heart. *And when you come for me, I'll be ready for you, Nana. I may even come for you first. My heart is so strong, filled with stories and love. And whatever you might have to use against me, I know you don't have that.*

A chorus of squeals and coos broke Sophie from her thoughts of her grandmother, and she looked up to see Syrena beating her tail, swimming joyfully into the pod of beluga whales who welcomed her. The water of the Baltic seemed thinner, as if more of the sun could get through; the light lit up Sophie's world in a heavenly blue, light as the sky. Flat-bodied flounders lay in the sand beneath her, looking upward with goofy eyes. A school of metallic silver fish shimmered past, momentarily blinding her. When her eyes adjusted, she could see the mermaid, one hand on the flank of a whale, the other beckoning her into the deep.

Acknowledgments

The author would like to thank Andi Winnette, her tireless editor at McSweeney's, as well as Sam Riley and Gabrielle Gantz for their work on the book, and everyone else at McS HQ who has helped to get this book out into the world. Thank you to her agent Lindsay Edgecombe for being so great all the time, and to those whose strong support of *Mermaid in Chelsea Creek* has made continuing the series a reality. Finally, an enormous thank you to illustrator Amanda Verwey for imagining the world of this book with such fantastic skill and creativity.

About the Author

Michelle Tea is the author of memoirs, novels, and poetry, as well as, most recently, the essay collection *How to Grow Up*. She is the founder and executive director of RADAR Productions, a literary nonprofit, and editor of Sister Spit Books, an imprint of City Lights. She is a former writer of horoscopes and a current reader of tarot cards.

About the Illustrator

Amanda Verwey is an illustrator and cartoonist based in Los Angeles. She has published four comic books, has a short story in the *QU33R* anthology (Northwest Press, 2014), and her illustrations are featured in the opening credits of the *Valencia* movie. She is a graduate of the Mills College Book Art Program. You can see more of her work at *amandamakescomics.com*.

COMING IN 2016 FROM
McSWEENEY'S McMULLENS

CASTLE
ON THE
RIVER
VISTULA

THE CAPTIVATING
FINALE OF THE
CHELSEA TRILOGY